Cut Flowers

love

Aneeta

Visit my website at www.aneeta.com

Cut Flowers

Aneeta Prem

Published in Great Britain by Prem Publishing

Copyright © Aneeta Prem 2016

Aneeta Prem asserts her moral right to be identified as the author of this work

A catalogue record of this book is available from the British Library

Edited by Colette Cherry

Illustrations by Robyn Neild

Set in Avenir

First Published in Great Britain 2016

Printed and bound in Great Britain by Page Bros Ltd, Mile Cross Lane, Norwich, NR6 6SA

ISBN Number 978-0-9569751-5-7

DEDICATION

I come from a family who give me unconditional love and support and I dedicate this book to them.

My loving gorgeous mum Savita Prem.

Chandra Shekhar Prem, my amazing dad, his spirit continues to guide me to fight for freedom.

Vineeta Prem Thornhill, my sensational sister.

My darling nephew Rishi Prem Thornhill.

I would also like to dedicate Cut Flowers to all those that have suffered FGM.

If you want to write a book to help saves lives and you can't spell, have given up with full stops and capital letters, and all you want to do is write down your stream of consciousness, then you need a huge support network.

When I was asked if I would write a book on FGM, I said I would only do it if I could lie on the sofa with a roaring fire and be fed treats in the way of my mum's delicious cooking.

Many people have helped this book along its way, and I particularly want to thank:

Robyn Neild – an amazingly talented illustrator. The characters you have drawn have really brought the story to life and I know everyone will love them as much as I do.

Lydia Wooldridge for the hours and days spent with me patiently listening and typing as we saw the story develop.

The University of Winchester for their help and support, and especially to Colette Cherry, Assistant Vice-Chancellor, for a huge amount of work not only editing, but for your patience, generosity and kindness.

Miriam Margolyes for writing such a brave and honest foreword and for telling it like it is.

The team at Reed Smith for all their help and support.

Thank you to:
Steven Walsh
Miranda Smith
Nick Boddington
The Secretary of State for Education, The RH Nicky Morgan MP
Baroness Jenny Jones
Lord Toby Harris
Nazir Afzal OBE
Kim, Lynne, Sue, Mits, Frankie, Richard, William-Tski and everyone else who has helped.
Thank you Vineeta, for reading the characters and for all your funny voices and not moaning too much that I cannot spell and have given up on writing in sentences.

Mum for her 100% support and love in everything I do.

And finally to Tony for the endless sacrifices helping to keep the dream alive for a book that we believe will save lives.

"Female genital mutilation is rightly a huge concern, and educating children and young people on how to keep themselves and others safe in the face of the abhorrent practice is essential. We are delighted to have worked with the Freedom Charity to develop 'Cut Flowers' and an accompanying PSHE lesson which we hope will be used by PSHE teachers across the country".

Joe Hayman
Chief Executive, PSHE Association

"'Cut Flowers' and Aneeta Prem's previous book, 'But it's not Fair', together provide a vital resource for children, young people and professionals on tackling these serious child abuse practices.

The story of the parallel lives of two young girls' summer holiday experiences where one is blighted by the real threat of FGM in the name of 'culture' and 'tradition' brilliantly underlines why all young girls must be safeguarded from violence and abuse. Schools have an important role in educating children, young people and staff on the damaging effects of FGM. The information and lesson plans appended to the book will provide a much needed resource for teachers and other professionals to support their work in educating against this brutal crime."

Chris Keates (Ms)
General Secretary, NASUWT The Teachers' Union

"The mutilation of young girls is a subject difficult to talk about, let alone write about. It's essential, however, that we do. This excellent book tells us what it is, how it impacts and how it can be stopped. Educating us all is the key to wiping this outrage off the face of the earth and 'Cut Flowers' plays an important part in that mission. I recommend it wholeheartedly."

Nazir Afzal OBE
Former Chief Prosecutor, Chief Executive of the Police & Crime Commissioners for England & Wales

"What a beautiful story!!! I found some parts provoked tears to my eyes as I could identify with some of the descriptions as a result of the experiences women have shared with me.

A beautifully written portrayal of an unexpected situation where a girl called Katie finds herself and her female relatives at risk of FGM by those she loves and trusts during a summer vacation. The characters are so real and tell the story of so many FGM survivors I have listened to and cared for over the years. This book tackles the entrenched secrecy and sorrow that FGM provokes. FGM has been introduced and described in such an empowering way that from the beginning you feel that whether you are a child, teenager or adult, you have the power to STOP FGM with the right support. This book helps equip readers to eradicate FGM in one generation."

Georgina Sosa
MSc, BA (Hons), RM, RGN, FGM Specialist, Midwife PhD

"Aneeta Prem's novel 'But It's Not Fair' had a profound effect on me and the students at our school. Aneeta has an extraordinary gift for taking subjects that are so often left unspoken and easily ignored, and then bringing them into sharp, unforgettable focus. 'Cut Flowers' does just the same - presenting the shocking subject of female genital mutilation in a style that is compellingly readable and, as a result, all the more disturbing. This is an important book. Recommended."

Geoff Barton
Head teacher, King Edward VI School

"Aneeta is a fantastic storyteller, a charming book with a powerful message - we can all help to end FGM."

Becca Naylor
Pro Bono Manager, Reed Smith

"Our group have all read Cut Flowers by Aneeta Prem. It is a game changer. Its sensitive and authentic. Had this book been around when we were growing up, maybe no one would have had to go through FGM. Men and boys must read this book too so they can understand the issues. Thank you Aneeta for your book on FGM. Its the best thing out there. Read it, understand it and stop it !!!"

FGM Survivors group London

"'Cut Flowers' is an essential read on FGM that will help potential victims and their friends to identify the signs and know where to go for help. The book will help the police gain a greater understanding of the issues involved in this dishonour crime and to help protect and bring about successful prosecutions."

Commander Mak Chishty
Lead on FGM, The National Police Chiefs' Council (NPCC)

"Cut flowers is a very powerful novel, it provides very useful and needed information to service users and their families. About the laws, access to care, information and advise".

Dr Comfort Momoh MBE
FGM and public health specialist

"This book doesn't always make for comfortable reading. It tackles some really difficult issues – the trauma of FGM, the problems of challenging culture and tradition, and the dilemma of protecting siblings from the well-meaning but misguided intentions of their parents.
It does this sensitively and tactfully, by telling the stories of our heroine Katie and her best friend Sophia. Through their eyes, we are introduced to the complex issues surrounding FGM and the controversy it can cause within families.

Perhaps most importantly, this book highlights how important it is to have support. If you have experienced FGM or know someone who has, don't be afraid to ask for help - whether it's family, friends, a teacher or the police. You don't need to deal with this on your own."

Professor Joy Carter DL
Vice-Chancellor, University of Winchester

"NAHT is pleased to support this latest contribution to the growing awareness of the need to confront and challenge FGM. We applaud Aneeta's creativity in presenting the issues to young people in the form of a novel and the potential this provides for schools to tackle the issue in a sensitive yet rigorous manner".

Russell Hobby, General Secretary of the NAHT, and Louis Coiffait, *CEO of NAHT Edge, (National Association of Head Teachers)*

FOREWORD

BY MIRIAM MARGOLYES

Let us be clear what this book is about – Female Genital Mutilation (FGM). A grim and ghastly practice which, whatever the 'cultural imperatives', must be totally outlawed. It is already illegal in the UK and should be stopped everywhere. FGM is a procedure traditionally carried out by a woman with no medical training. Anaesthetics and antiseptic treatments are not generally used and the practice is usually carried out using unsterilised sharp implements, many of them old and crude, leading to serious and often life-threatening infections.

There are no health benefits to FGM. Removing and damaging healthy and normal female genital tissue interferes with the natural functions of girls' and women's bodies.

I wanted to lay out before you the unvarnished horror of this procedure, so that no one can be in any doubt of its brutality and perilous results.

But this is a tradition deeply embedded in the culture of many Asian, African and Middle Eastern nations. Authorities in the UK have become aware that schoolgirls are being sent home in the holidays to be cut, often by family members. These children have no idea of what they face when they leave the UK for their longed-for 'African Adventure'.

This book shows what can happen to a perfectly normal immigrant family who have settled completely happily into the English way of life. It uses the clever device of showing parallel summer holidays: one the typical beach vacation – ice creams and children playing at the seaside. The other a seemingly magnificent visit to the ancestral African village, and what lies in wait for Katie, our heroine, as the ceremony for the cut is planned by her aunt.

All the characters are real and recognisable and fun, speaking like modern kids, full of life, joyous and naughty. The grown-ups, both in England and in Africa, are believable and likeable. Even Granny

JoJo, the formidable 'African queen', has a depth and honesty which removes any taint of racist criticism from her.

It's a good story, with a serious point. But the life and energy of the characters removes any didactic cloud from what is an essential problem, to be faced and extinguished. This book will help young people better understand what may be a very real threat to themselves, their sister or their friends, and offers suggestions of how they can get the help they may urgently need.

Miriam Margolyes OBE   Photo credit: Jennifer Robertson

Born in Oxford, Miriam is a veteran of stage and screen. Winner of the BAFTA Best Supporting Actress award in 1993 for The Age of Innocence, Best Supporting Actress at the 1989 LA Critics Circle Awards for her role in Little Dorrit and a Sony Radio Award for Best Actress in 1993 for 'Oliver Twist'.

She has starred and featured in countless films, TV shows, radio shows and commercials, but readers will probably know her best as the much-loved Professor Sprout in the Harry Potter film series.

"Freedom does vital work by helping to give schools the tools they need to ensure every girl has the opportunity to fulfil their potential and help pupils understand that violence against women and girls will not be tolerated."

Freedom is an inspirational charity and the work of Aneeta and her team to support teachers and pupils is helping to ensure every young person feels safe and has the opportunity to fulfil their potential.

FGM is a terrible crime. It destroys lives and causes extreme and lifelong suffering to women and girls. This is a serious issue and this Government is committed to ending this abusive and illegal practice.

That is why we have taken bold action to ensure that awareness of FGM is greater now than ever before. We have significantly strengthened the law to better protect victims and ensure perpetrators are brought to justice. We have expanded the data that we are collecting across the NHS, and strengthened safeguarding responsibilities in order to better protect and care for those exposed to this horrific abuse.

Education also plays a crucial role. Young people must understand that FGM is not tolerated in our society. Schools up and down the country are helping to create an open and supportive environment by having high quality personal, social, and health education.

I hope that there comes a day when we no longer need to talk about FGM, as it becomes a thing of the past, and that every young girl across the world grows up free from fear and violence."

Secretary of State for Education and Minister for Women and Equalities The Rt Hon Nicky Morgan

Dear Reader,

I hope you enjoy reading Cut Flowers.

In case you're wondering, it's not about gardening.

It's about an issue that affects more than 70 million girls and women around the world.

I have based the story on things that have really happened and even while you're reading this someone is going through FGM.

If anything in here is affecting you please tell someone; a teacher or the police.

Doing nothing isn't an option.

I thought it might help if I introduced the characters to you, They are listed on the next page.

Enjoy reading.

I'm off to play with my darling dog Deeva.

Love, your friend,

Katie

Tall and lean with an athletic build would be too simple a way to describe Katie. An 11-year-old going on 30 is how Rose, her mum, describes her. Katie has big hazel eyes like her dad and beautiful wavy black hair that, if her mum didn't put relaxer on, would be a bit wiry. She is bright and academic, into IT, good at sport, well spoken and doesn't talk back!

Sophia

Sophia is 11 years old, slim and small, with long, dark hair that has grown past her waist. She's loud, uninhibited and excitable, gets annoyed easily, very curious and demands to be the centre of attention. She is into fashion and obsessed by celebrities, and the highlight of her week is watching Britain's Got Talent on Saturday night. Sophia's favourite saying is 'But it's not fair!' She says it all the time and it's now her catchphrase.

Lizzie

Katie's sister is 6 years old, petite, with mid-length brown curly hair. She takes after her father. She is the baby of the family and into everything pink.

Benji

Katie's brother is 10 years old, football mad and the tallest in his class. He loves computer games, chocolates and sweets, and playing tricks on everyone in the family. He spends his whole time playing outside and although his mum Rose tries to get him to do schoolwork, tidy his room and have a wash, she's losing the battle with him.

Rose

Katie's mum is in her late 30s, very bossy and controlling. She is large-boned and very tall with quite a stern face, but she is pretty when she smiles. Her hair is tied into a neat ponytail swept back off her dark-skinned face with brown eyes. She is a qualified nurse and a popular school governor.

Steve (Katie's dad)

Steve has brown hair that is a little short and just starting to thin. He is an IT guru, very technical and easy-going to the extent it seems like he is almost asleep! He is very dominated by his wife Rose who spends her whole time leaving him endless lists of DIY jobs around the house and is happy spending all his time playing with the latest gadgets.

Granny Jojo

Katie's grandmother and Rose's mum is a strong, powerful woman almost 6ft tall. Time has not withered her strong frame and her hands, although elegant, are large. They are working hands and have milked thousands of goats over the years.

Vinny

Sophia's sister is five years older than her and Sophia thinks she is a right goody-two-shoes and their mum's favourite. Vinny can cook whole meals from scratch, even making round rotis. She is very pretty and filled out in all the right places. She's also very clever and loves reading, although she's actually really easy-going.

Jasmine

Sophia's mum is really young and pretty. She cooks great food, but because her mum died when she was small, she never learned to do mum things. She does not read her children stories or make them fairy cakes. She works all the time, even on Saturday mornings. She is very supportive of Vinny and Sophia as well as trying to hold on to her youth.

Shekhar

Sophia's dad is pretty cool and liberal. He is outspoken about politics and has spent his life fighting injustice. He does translating work at the Council but loves home life. He knows how to fix things. Sophia has his genes for exaggerating stories.

Next Door Aunty – NDA

NDA has a plump round face, white hair, soft features and watery blue eyes. She lives alone as she was widowed young, but is down-to-earth with a great sense of humour. She adores her grandson Charlie.

Charlie

NDA's grandson is 12 years old with floppy brown hair that turns a golden blond in the sun. Charlie is a bit of a handful, especially since his parents' divorce. His hairstyle has been the same since he was 2 when his dad Ray cut it using a pudding basin as a guide. Charlie has always hated the hairdresser because he believes that if he gets his hair cut he would lose his strength, a bit like Samson. He's into everything and surprised everyone when he turned out to be a natural piano player. When his parents moved house when he was 3, they inherited a rather grand piano. To everyone's delight he managed to play it almost instinctively.

William Payne
The owner of the caravan park that Sophia, Charlie and NDA stay at for a week is a jolly chap, very sociable and larger than life in his late 50s. He is 6ft tall and almost 6ft wide, with a beer-belly, red nose, large face, theatrical moustache and greying hair. He loves his food and fine wine.

Kai – Rose's younger brother, 6ft 3in and a modern man of his time.

Lily – Rose's older sister, very similar to Rose.

Ivy – Kai's wife. Very superstitious and into alternative healing and rituals.

Katie
21 September
A secondary school on a sunny day

Almost every morning one of Sophia's school friends would be subject to her usual moan, 'But it's not fair; if we didn't have to go to assembly we could get to school almost an hour later.'

Today was different; Katie was excited about the assembly. There was an air of anticipation – not least as today the subject was the experience of several different generations.

Katie whispers, 'Now we can help save someone's life.'

Sophia smiles reassuringly and whispers back, 'No one would believe that your own family, people you love, you trust, could take you on a supposed holiday and...'

'It's been going on in my family for generations', Katie whispers back, her voice trembling. 'They believed it was alright for me to be brutally cut, changing me forever. They believed that it was OK for me to grow up never feeling like a complete woman. Sophia, if the other kids know about it, they could stop it happening.

'Today's important; do you think the kids will get it?' Katie asks shakily.

'I can't see how anyone could fail to understand, especially with you telling it. You're the cleverest person in our school,' Sophia beams.

'I know I'm not, but that's kind of you. Wow, thank goodness I've got you as a friend to help me through this.'

A whole school assembly is very rare, but today the hall is packed with an array of important guests sitting at the front including all the school governors, star reporter Ros Irwin and the complete Freedom team. There are hundreds of gold and coloured books laid out across the front of the hall stage, all gleaming like jewels. Sophia takes centre stage as the school choir sing her award-winning Freedom song. Deeva, the head of Freedom Charity, clears her throat, pats her microphone and beams at everyone.

'It's a real honour to have been invited to your school today. We want to thank Vinny, one of our Freedom Ambassadors, for asking us to talk to you about the horrific practice of Female Genital Mutilation and encouraging you all to download the Freedom Charity app. And a special well done to you all, as you are the school that has the most Freedom app downloads to date.'

She continues, 'The World Health Organisation estimates that between 100 and 140 million girls and women have been subject to FGM. That's more than all the women currently living in the USA! It is estimated that three million girls in Africa alone are at risk of undergoing FGM. It gives me great pleasure to ask Katie Smith to give us some more facts and figures about this awful practice.'

As Katie starts to speak there is silence, and everyone sits very still. Katie tells them about her summer and the hairs on the back of the necks of several teachers stand up.

As the assembly draws to an end, the head of Freedom rounds up the assembly by saying, 'Katie Smith, an ordinary girl from a local school, is determined to stop FGM in her lifetime.'

Everyone claps and cheers, and Sophia smiles and hugs Katie.

1

Hurray, Last Day of School!

21 July 2016
Katie and Sophia

'I hate stupid, smelly, stinky school, and I think I might not like Miss Adams after today either. It's not fair having to do stupid presentations about our summer holidays.'

Sophia turns to Katie saying, 'It's alright for you, you're going abroad for your vacation, but I'm staying here for a boring staycation. What on earth will my presentation be about? Staying in the flat all day? Mind you, I could train Vinny to make breakfast in bed, and then I could watch daytime TV. I could have the remote all to myself and flick channels all day without everyone moaning. Maybe it's not so bad!'

Then she remembers, 'Of course NDA is taking me away for a week. The only downside is sharing her with her grandson Charlie. He's only coming 'cos NDA feels so sorry for him now his mum's going on honeymoon and his dad's at work. He can't stay by himself, so he'll be at the caravan too, worse luck.' NDA stands for Next Door Aunty, which is what Sophia's family call their neighbour.

Katie is in a hurry. 'Oooh sorry Sophia, I've got to run. I'm meeting Mum at the school gates. I'll call you at home later.'

Sophia calls out behind her, half-muttering to herself, 'You might have to get me on NDA's mobile. I'll be round there after school. It's not fair that I haven't got my own phone.'

The school gate is still busy with everyone piling out. Sophia waits there, hoping that her older sister Vinny with her friends Abi and Minny will walk home with her. Sophia's bag is so heavy she is hoping that she can beg Vinny to carry it home for her.

When she turns up at NDA's, Sophia is in a grumpy mood because she has had to struggle home on her own. But within seconds of tucking into tea and NDA's homemade scones everything seems much better. NDA always knows how to cheer Sophia up.

2

The School Run

21 July, outside the school
Katie

Katie's mum Rose stands at the next-door primary school gate with Katie's younger sister Lizzie who is wearing the blue and gold glittery Egyptian mask she has just made in class. Katie instantly realises this will frustrate their mum, as the glitter is already showing signs of falling off. In fact, little Lizzie's uniform is already covered in tiny specks of the blue and gold glitter.

Lizzie shouts over excitedly, 'Katie, Katie!'

Rose is deep in conversation about cyber-safety and parental supervision of the internet with the other members of the Parent Teacher Association at the school gate. She is a parent governor at the school, and so always ends up holding court and delivering impromptu safeguarding meetings. Little Lizzie strains away from her, rushing to see Katie. As always, Benji is five minutes behind everyone else and is doing keepie-uppies as he walks. His school shoes are becoming more and more scuffed with every kick and no amount of polishing will get them back to normal. Benji's least favourite job in the morning is polishing the dreaded school shoes. Benji runs to Katie, desperate to tell her about his new keepie-uppie record,

'I can do 36 all in one go, Katie!'

'Wow Benji, that's fab. My record currently stands at 15. You can do over double that!' Katie marvels.

Looking directly at Benji, Rose quietly yet firmly says in a low voice, 'School shoes!'

Katie turns to Benji and says, 'You know Mum's going to tell you off later. You really shouldn't be kicking the ball around in your school shoes!'

Rose finally finishes talking, looks down at her phone to check the time and says, 'Come on, let's go. Benji will be late for football practice. I'm going to drop you off at football training en route as we're so late.'

She opens her enormous Mary Poppins-style bag and hands him a bottle of water and a banana. 'That'll keep you going till dinner time.'

Lizzie holds Katie's hand and is skipping alongside, as her stride isn't as big as Katie's yet. Katie and Benji are both the tallest in their classes as they have inherited their mother's 'tall' gene. Little Lizzie always pesters the others to stretch her, as she wants to be as tall as they are. Despite Katie and Benji's best attempts at joke-stretching Lizzie, it hasn't made any difference – Lizzie definitely takes after her father. The game always ends up with the pair swinging Lizzie while she squeals in delight.

As Rose and Benji approach the football field they catch sight of Josh's mum. The boys have been friends for years and have attended summer football camp together since they were five.

 Josh's mum calls over, 'Hiya Rose, is it still OK for Benji to come to tea before we drop him back?'

Rose looks over and shouts back, 'Yes, that sounds great, Caroline.' Turning to Benji she quietly says, 'But don't forget your homework.'

Rose says a bit too loudly, 'Be well behaved for Josh's mother.'

Benji and Josh mutter under their breaths, '…and tidy your room, and put the bins out, and polish your shoes.'

Both boys laugh and run off. Benji being a shoeshine has been a long-standing joke between the two of them.

Josh's parents are ultra-cool. Josh has a 42-inch TV in his room and last Christmas his dad bought him two rocking gaming chairs with drink holders.

If Benji could he would spend every minute at Josh's house.

'It's not fair', Benji complained to Josh.

'My mum makes me do everything. I have to clean my room and even have to put my washing in the laundry basket'.

'You've not trained them right', Josh said sincerely.

'Look – you're the number one son and you've got to make it clear you don't do housework! Your time is too valuable and when you're signed by a premiership football club you'll buy her a big house and you will employ cleaners but for now she's got to do it'.

Benji had once tried that line with his mum and was grounded for a week.

Normally Katie would now be dropped off at tennis en route but the afternoon lessons have finished for the summer holidays. At the tennis club's annual awards dinner, Katie won the club trophy for most improved forehand. Unfortunately, this year she won't be able to go to tennis camp during the holidays because of the 'Big African Adventure'.

Rose, Katie and Lizzie return home and as they walk up the drive Katie dusts off the glitter-covered Lizzie to prevent glitter getting everywhere inside the house.

As they enter the house, Rose says to Katie, 'Take Lizzie straight into the utility room and get her changed. I don't want glitter getting everywhere.'

Katie replies, 'What, you want me to hoover her down, Mum?' She grabs the cordless vacuum and starts hoovering Lizzie.

'Really Katie?! Come on, get her changed and get upstairs,' Rose exclaims before heading into the kitchen and pouring the girls a glass of milk each.

Katie sighs contentedly, 'It's great; I don't have any homework tonight. Miss Adams says we've worked so hard all year, we deserve a break for the end of term.'

3

Recycling

21 July 6pm, Sophia's house
Sophia

Sophia and NDA walk together next door to Sophia's flat where Dad and Mum are preparing a special treat, something they make a couple of times a week – aloo and pea parathas with natural yogurt.

Everyone adores parathas, a flatbread stuffed with potatoes and peas, made with atta (whole-wheat flour). The whole flat is filled with the delicious aroma of fried bread. Dad substitutes ghee for olive oil to make the parathas slightly healthier!

INGREDIENTS
Potato mix
- *4 large potatoes*
- *1 large onion*
- *1 tsp. of coriander seeds*
- *A pinch of salt*
- *A pinch of chilli powder*
- *A handful of petits pois peas*

Chapatti mix
- *2 cups of atta / wholewheat flour*
- *1 or 2 tsp. of ghee or olive oil*
- *½ tsp. of salt*
- *Water as required for kneading*
- *Olive oil or ghee for frying*

Peel and boil the potatoes. Then mash them. Let them cool and then add finely chopped onion, cumin seeds, freshly chopped coriander, salt and chilli powder to taste. Mix well.

Mix the chapatti flour with water and knead into a ball. Leave to rest for half an hour (that's the dough, not you!)

Break off a small amount of dough and roll into 15cm circle (approximately).

Then make your mash. Mix into a ball. Add to the centre of your 15cm dough circle and wrap the dough around the mix.

Dust the work surface with flour and gently roll out the dough and mash ball. The circle should have a diameter of 15cm.

Put a small drizzle of oil (either ghee or olive oil) on a tavar (a flat frying pan). Cook slowly on the hob. Cook on both sides until golden brown.

Add a knob of butter, get a plate, eat and **enjoy!**

An hour later, the flat is bustling full of noise with everyone talking all at once between mouthfuls of Mum and Dad's delicious feast. Then Sophia and Vinny tidy away the dirty plates before the daily dose of EastEnders.

As they sit in the front room, Sophia moans, 'I hate school, it's just not fair!'

Dad looks up, his eyes wide with concern, 'Why darling? What's happened?'

'You're not being bullied are you?' Mum asks anxiously.

'Bet you're in trouble for not doing your homework!' Vinny scoffs.

'Neither,' NDA pipes in. 'No, our dear Sophia hates school because she has summer holiday homework.'

In a flash Mum and Dad's sympathy vanishes.

'Oh Sophia,' Dad says as he shakes his head, 'I was worried for a second.'

'But it's not fair! Homework in the holidays is just wrong on every level,' Sophia replies.

Everyone laughs and shouts out Sophia's catchphrase, 'But it's not fair!'

Sophia pokes out her tongue and is about to say something rude, but she knows it isn't worth it. Dad looks slightly worried as she storms out of the room in a huff.

'Oh dear, I'd better go after her.' Dad always hates it if any of his girls are upset. But within seconds Sophia bursts back in, saying, 'I've sorted it out!'

'How?' Mum looks confused.

Sophia is holding an old schoolbook.

'Listen everyone,' she says before reading out pages from an old school project, All About Me.

'My name is Sophia. I live at home with my mum Jasmine, my dad Shekhar, and my lanky, loony sister Vinny. We practically live with my Next Door Aunty, whose name is Grace Swan. She's not my real Aunty but I wish she were. I've got really long hair that goes down past my waist and I have to be really careful when I go to the toilet that it doesn't get wet....'

'I just have to tweak it a little and it's done. It's called recycling,' Sophia says proudly.

'It's called cheating and none of my girls are cheats, are they?' Dad says sternly.

Vinny giggles away quietly.

NDA smiles. 'Sophia, you are going to have tons to write about on our special week away, dear.'

Sophia nods, a little half-heartedly.

Mum goes into the kitchen and walks back a few minutes later with a tray of hot milky chocolate with squirty cream and cocoa sprinkled on top. She even has Kit Kats for everyone!

'Drink up Sophia, I'm sure it's your bedtime,' Mum smiles warmly.

'It's n..' Sophia couldn't finish the sentence before she is interrupted.

'Not fair,' everyone joins in. Even Sophia starts smiling. After goodnight kisses and lots of 'love yous', Sophia is sound asleep.

4

Packing

21 July 6pm, Katie's house
Katie

Before her mum has a chance to comment on Katie's lack of homework, Katie says, 'Do you think you could ask Dad if I can take his new SLR camera?'

'I can't make any promises Katie, but we'll ask Dad when he gets home,' Rose sensibly replies and then, turning to Katie, adds, 'But seeing as you've finished all your homework, let's crack on with packing. Once that's done, you can start your new book. Katie, go get the luggage organiser bags out of the cupboard, please.'

Katie collects the mesh bags. Rose has allocated the children two colour-coordinated bags each; socks, pants and vests in one; shorts and t-shirts in the other.

Lizzie shouts out, 'Can I have the pink ones please?'

'You MAY have the pink ones,' Rose replies.

'Thanks Mum! Pink has always been my favourite colour.'

The three of them head upstairs and the girls jump on Rose's bed. Rose goes into her cupboard and pulls out a large brown paper bag. Katie's eyes light up in anticipation. Rose excitedly tips a mountain of clothes onto the bed.

'Look at all those colours,' she says. She puts Benji's clothes to one side – she only really needs to pack him a football top and shorts; he normally refuses to wear anything else – and proceeds to show the girls theirs. Katie helps Lizzie into a beautiful pink cotton dress and afterwards she puts on her own brilliant white one.

'They're so beautiful, Mum. Thank you,' Katie says quietly.

Both girls rush to Rose who is sitting at the end of the bed admiring her beautiful daughters. The girls swing their arms around her and give her a big kiss.

'You're going to look so pretty for Granny Jojo,' Rose says proudly.

Immediately after, she urges the girls to get out of their new clothes. 'Come on, girls, we don't want to spoil the new dresses. Let's get them packed away neatly in the organiser bags.'

Dad walks through the door just as dinner is being served. He's panting as the tube was late and he has had to rush back. He gives them all a kiss and turns to the girls asking how their last day at school had gone.

Katie excitedly says, 'Everyone has been asked to do this big presentation in September about our summer holiday. Dad, do you think I could borrow your camera, so I've got some excellent photos for my African Adventure presentation?'

Dad looks at Rose and she gives him the nod of approval. 'Yes, Katie – great idea, on condition that your mum looks after the camera when you're not using it.'

5

Getting Ready to Leave

22 July 2pm, Katie's house
Katie and Sophia

'Katie, quick come down, Sophia's on the phone for you,' Rose shouts up the stairs.

'Coming, thanks Mum,' Katie replies.

'Katie, it's me, Sophia. How's the first day of the hols been? I didn't get up till 11 o'clock and unfortunately I didn't get breakfast in bed. Vinny is going to need some serious training – this can't go on all summer! I've been watching the music channel back-to-back and I'm going to start practising my dance moves and singing. I've got a lot of competitions to win.'

Sophia's voice suddenly drops, 'Katie, I'm a bit worried about the new school project. How are you going to do yours?'

Katie says thoughtfully, 'You've got so much going on this summer, why don't you just keep a diary? You could always turn it into a video blog at the end. I'm going to do the same. I'll compile all the film and photos I shoot in Africa and turn it into a slideshow. We could always work on them together. I'm sure my dad would help us with the editing, he does this sort of thing all the time.'

Sophia says excitedly, 'Fantastic! Do you think he can put it on YouTube for us? We'll be famous before you know it.'

'My holiday has been a little different to yours' says Katie. 'Unlike you, I had to get up really early. Mum's given us a massive list of jobs to do before we can leave tomorrow. And Mum keeps arguing with Benji. He's insisting on taking an enormous suitcase. I bet he fills it with footballs!'

'She's whizzing around like a whirlwind at the moment,' Katie explains.

On cue, Katie's mum shouts down the stairs, frustrated, 'Katie, come on! There's so much to get through.'

Sophia hurriedly says, 'Have a fabulous time, Katie. Take lots of photos and tell me all about it when you get back. You can always

WhatsApp me on Vinny's phone if you want!'

Katie replies, 'You too, Sophia, have a great time. Don't forget, you must keep this diary. You'll need to gather lots of info for the presentation.'

6

Train Journey

9 August 10am
Sophia

'I'm so-oo bored, are we nearly there yet?' Sophia whines to NDA.

'We've just pulled out of the station. We've got three hours before we arrive. Remember I showed you on the map? We only left London five minutes ago,' NDA chuckles.

'I'm so-oo bored,' Sophia huffs. She suddenly spies the bag of goodies on the seat next to NDA.

With a glint in her eye, Sophia wheedles, 'I'm so-oo hungry,' as she theatrically raises the back of her hand to her forehead and sighs, 'Do you reckon there is something for me to eat?'

NDA chuckles warmly, 'Oh dear, you are my drama queen! Ahh we can't have you wasting away.'

NDA then pulls out the largest Tupperware box known to mankind and Sophia hurriedly gets out the kitchen roll in anticipation. She starts unwinding sheets and sheets of white paper. Before she gets too far NDA swiftly retrieves the kitchen roll and tears off two squares for them both. NDA opens the magic Tupperware box and pulls out two huge cubes of silver foil. She passes one package to Sophia and she carefully unwraps each corner for her, to reveal a massive doorstop sarnie. It looks as if NDA has used half a loaf of bread just to make one sandwich.

Sophia gently pulls the enormous slices apart and squeals excitedly, 'Yes, butter and jam – my favourite.'

NDA always makes the best sandwiches. The bread is always caked in a thick layer of butter and covered with lashings of her homemade strawberry jam. Sophia always picks the whole strawberries out of the jam and eats them first before tackling the rest.

NDA smiles warmly and says, 'You wouldn't get away with that at home! I put extra strawberries in because I know how much you love them.'

She leans into her big bag and pulls out an old-fashioned checked thermos flask, and Sophia asks politely, 'May I have a cup please?'

Peace and tranquillity fill the carriage for ten minutes, until Sophia finishes her last mouthful…. She screws up the ball of foil and starts throwing it up in the air to catch.

NDA quietly says, 'I think there's a bin at the top of the carriage and that's where that ball belongs!'

Sophia marches straight up to the bin and back again. Realising she would like to explore, she asks NDA, 'Can I wander round the train?'

NDA replies, 'Yes, so long as you don't pester anyone!'

A few minutes later Sophia returns in an excited state,

'NDA, guess what, there's first class! There's plenty of space, why don't we go? They don't have thermos flasks; they get free tea! We might even spot a celebrity or two.' As she tries to get hold of the bags, Sophia says, 'Come on, come on. I'm sure the guards will move our cases down for us.'

An amused NDA shakes her head and says, 'Darling, you have to pay a lot extra for that!' Gently pulling Sophia's arm she says, 'Ah we can't be doing with that first class. I'd need a mortgage for a ticket. Come and sit down. You can have a look at some of my magazines.'

Sophia slouches into the seat, 'Ahh, it's not fair! Are we nearly there yet?' NDA pulls out four magazines.

Sophia scans through them in thirty seconds and shouts out, 'Finished! Any more?'

NDA quietly says to her, 'Oooh you can't have finished them already. Did you check the competitions in the back? You're meant to be winning us all these competitions,' she teases.

Sophia is suddenly enthused and flicks through all the magazines again. There are so many competitions to enter, she can't decide which one to pick.

She turns to NDA and says, 'Can you help me?'

NDA says, 'Try this one. All you have to do is write a limerick!'

'What's a limerick?' Sophia eagerly responds. NDA spontaneously bursts into rhyme:

There was a young girl on the train,
Who ended up being a pain,
She walked all around,
And wouldn't sit down,
So we flushed that pain right down the drain!'

Sophia has her own go at composing a limerick:

NDA gave the guard a big kiss,
But he moved his big head so she missed,
She became really pi**ed.

NDA quickly interrupts, 'That's enough of that! I'll be washing your mouth out with soap and water!'

As the train finally pulls up at the station, Sophia and NDA are right by the door, desperate to get off. Just past the barrier NDA spies her son Graham. He rushes over to hug his mum and take her bags. Sophia runs up to him with open arms, but just before reaching him, shyness takes over and she runs back to NDA's side.

NDA's grandson Charlie is sitting in the front passenger seat with his feet on the seat and one finger firmly stuck up his nose. Sophia instantly thinks he looks like Horrid Henry with his mop of uncontrollable blond hair.

Graham opens the front door and shoos Charlie to the back, 'Oi you, get in the back.'

Automatically Charlie retorts, 'But it's not fair.'

Sophia bursts into laughter and NDA says, 'Who does that remind you of?'

NDA ruffles Charlie's hair and tries to kiss him. Charlie squirms away. He looks at Sophia and says, 'Whiskers, urgh.'

She points at his fingers and says, 'Bogeys, urghhh!' They both fall about laughing for the whole journey to the caravan site.

NDA turns to her son Graham, 'I told you it'd be a good idea to bring this one along' she says pointing at Sophia. 'Charlie will have someone to play around with when you head back to work tonight.'

Graham nods in agreement, 'You're going to have your hands full. Will you be able to handle this pair when I've gone back to work?'

As they approach the caravan, NDA says, 'I'm dying for a cuppa tea, luv.' In the caravan she puts the kettle on and pulls out a tin of butterfly fairy cakes for them all to enjoy.

Charlie pesters his dad, 'Can't I have a Cola, Dad?'

'No you can't! Your granny has made tea for us all,' Graham replies.

NDA looks at Charlie and says, 'You're not going to be drinking that all week!'

Charlie moans back, 'But I'm so-oo hot'.

'Well, a cup of tea will cool you down!' NDA replies.

As soon as they finish their butterfly fairy cakes Charlie looks at Sophia and says, 'Come on, I'll race you to the sand dunes.'

He runs off shouting, 'I bet you can't keep up!'

Graham calls after the children, 'Don't forget I'm leaving in a couple of hours. Be back by then!'

7

Airport

23 July 7am
Katie

The family are all sitting in the departure lounge munching on doughnuts, a rare treat. Dad and Benji are competing to see who can eat a whole doughnut without licking their lips.

After finishing the doughnuts, Dad shows Katie how to set up the mini-tripod and work the self-timer function on the camera. The family all pose for a photograph. Rose has a big grin on her face and her arms around everyone, and Katie and Lizzie make half-doughnut smiles. Dad and Benji's doughnuts have already been scoffed, so all that remains are sugar-coated lips!

As per usual they are hours too early for the flight. They all decide to have a look round the airport and head into one of the shops. Benji is immediately drawn like a magnet to the biggest bar of Toblerone. It's pretty much the same size as Lizzie!

Benji loves chocolate and over the last few weeks has been doing extra jobs for extra pocket money so that he can fill his extra-large suitcase full of chocolate and sweets, mainly chewy jelly worms.

The only other thing Benji was saving his extra money for was jokes and tricks. He bought several plastic moving spiders and snakes and on the last day was thrilled that his fake lizard had arrived in time for him to pack in his suitcase to scare his granny and cousins.

He picks up the Toblerone, calls over to Rose with a cheeky, wistful grin on his face, 'Mmmuuuummmm?'

Rose quickly replies, 'No, come on Benji, let's have a look at the books over here.'

Both girls move to the soft toy section. Lizzie jumps up trying to reach an enormous tiger, and shouts, 'Look, there's Fremont the Freedom tiger!'

Katie lifts Lizzie up so she can grab hold of Fremont and at the same time she catches a glimpse of the new iWatch out of the corner of her eye.

Katie shouts excitedly, 'Look Dad, that's the same as your one.'

Dad replies, 'It's the latest model, Katie. It probably has more features.'

Katie looks at Dad with longing eyes, 'Ah, I wish I had one.'

At that moment Rose and Benji reappear. Benji eagerly agrees, 'Me too, me too.'

Mum encourages them to stop all the window-shopping, 'Come on, you!' And with that, she places Fremont back on the shelf. Dad spots Lizzie looking longingly at the line of Fremont tigers. He picks her up and throws her on his shoulders. Benji and Katie each have an arm around Dad's waist and the four of them all meander towards security with Rose walking alongside.

As the queues increase, Dad reluctantly says, 'Come on, I think you ought to go through now.' He turns to Benji, lifts him up for a hug and a kiss and says, 'Make sure you look after your mum and the girls.'

Benji beams with pride and suddenly feels very grown up. He quickly but sincerely replies, 'I promise I will, Dad!'

Dad then turns to Lizzie, 'Be really good for your mum.' She nods, gives him a big kiss and immediately starts crying.

Dad hurriedly kisses Katie and says, 'Enjoy your African Adventure, make the most of every opportunity – I know you will!'

Turning to Rose, he says affectionately, 'I'm going to miss you all so much, call me the second you land.'

The four of them head towards security and Dad shouts one final 'LOVE YOU' as they pass through.

On the plane, Rose fills the children's heads with stories of Granny Jojo and playing with the goats in the back field.

Benji asks, 'Why has Granny Jojo never been over to the UK?'

Rose responds, 'Well, you know what Granny Jojo always says…'

At this point both Benji and Katie chant in unison, 'If I were meant to fly, I'd have wings!'

A few hours later they touch down in Africa. The heat that welcomes them as they step off the plane stuns them all. The air is hot and exciting. Rose's heart sings at the thought of finally coming home and seeing her mother.

8

Caravan Staycation

9 August 5pm, caravan site
Sophia

A couple of hours later, laughter fills the caravan site as Sophia and Charlie return from the dunes. They rush into the caravan dropping sand everywhere as NDA tuts and tells them both to get changed. NDA thinks to herself, 'Keeping sand out of this caravan will be like shovelling snow while it's still snowing!'

Shortly after, Dad has to leave. He says his goodbyes and he pleads with Charlie, 'Pleeeeasssssseee be good for granny!'

NDA comments, 'If he's not, I'll be straight on the phone. Don't you worry!'

They wave goodbye and sit down to one of NDA's famous re-heated cauliflower cheese suppers.

The campsite owner, William Payne, taps at the door and opens it without waiting for a reply, 'Just checking everything's ok in here?!'

NDA looks at the man suspiciously and William responds, 'I'm the site owner.' Giving an over-emphasised wink, William continues, 'I'll give you a VIP tour later, if you want?'

NDA quickly retorts, 'I think we can find the way to the shower block and clubhouse ourselves thank you.'

'Hmmmm, something smells nice!', William adds, sniffing inquisitively.

Sophia chirps up, 'Yeh, it's NDA's absolutely scrumptious cauliflower cheese,' screwing her nose up as she says it.

William says hopefully, 'Ooooh, I am partial to a bit of cauli-cheese.'

NDA quickly intervenes, half-pushing him out of the door. 'Was there anything else?' As she closes the door firmly behind him, she looks at Sophia and Charlie and says, 'What a cheek!'

Much to NDA's amazement Sophia and Charlie are shattered from all the fresh sea air and they flop into their beds before the ten o'clock news.

9

Arrival into Africa

24 July
Katie

At the airport Uncle Kai and his wife Ivy are waiting with banners plastered with

Welcome Rose, Katie, Benji and Lizzie!

Uncle Kai is 6 foot 4 inches tall – even taller than Rose – and perhaps the tallest person the children have ever seen. Ivy is beautiful, tall and slim, and she is draped in a white shawl. The pair run over to the family, recognising the children from photos. As they all embrace, Uncle Kai hoists all three children up. In unison, they squeal with delight. The six of them pile into the car and start the two-hour journey to Granny Jojo's village. Rose chats to Ivy and Kai as they travel, while the children doze in the back. It had been an early start for them all and the children hadn't been able to sleep the night before, due to all the excitement.

Kai wakes up the children by shouting, 'Kids! Check this out. There's a croc over there in the lake! The first crocodile you will have seen in the wild.'

Benji replies excitedly, 'Can we get out, Uncle Kai? Please, please, let's get a closer look.'

Katie agrees, 'Yes, stop the car, Uncle Kai.'

Aunty Ivy turns round and jokingly says, 'Those beasts will eat you for breakfast and no amount of potion from the medicine man will get you back out! Even if we fed all three of you to them, they'd still be on the hunt for more. There just isn't enough meat on you kids!'

The kids laugh. Deep down they know how dangerous crocodiles could be – Rose has already lectured them at length about the dangers of wild animals. As the journey progresses, the sun begins to set. Gradually, the deep red sun takes up almost half the electric blue sky, getting redder and redder as it disappears. The car finally pulls into Granny Jojo's gates and Rose instantly recognises her mother, sitting on the veranda, from the faint outline cast by her figure. Granny Jojo has aged since Rose last saw her, but she is still a strong, powerful, tall woman. Excitement fills the car and everyone piles out as quickly as possible.

Granny Jojo is standing on the veranda now. She is almost 6 foot tall and time has not withered her strong frame. Her hands, although elegant are large. They are working hands and have milked thousands of goats over the years. Granny Jojo exclaims in joy, 'My babies have returned!'

Rose shouts, 'Mumma, I've brought your grandchildren home to you!'

Granny Jojo pulls the three of them to her. Rose falls to her knees in front of her mother, crying uncontrollably. She suddenly realises how much she has missed her mother and she is overwhelmed by the sorrow of her mother not being there for so many great life events: her marriage; the birth of her children; her qualifying as a nurse.

Granny Jojo raises Rose up and they embrace. At this point Rose composes herself quickly so she doesn't upset her children – they have never seen their mother like this before. They haven't appreciated what it must feel like to not see your family for over fifteen years.

'Right,' Granny Jojo says, 'looking at the size of you kids, it's clear your mother's cooking hasn't got any better since she left. Run inside, there's some rice and yam in the pot on the table.'

Granny Jojo turns to Lizzie and says, 'We'll have to put you in the ground and start watering you like the runner beans!'

Lizzie's bottom lip starts to quiver. Katie grabs her hand and says, 'She's only teasing. Come on, let's have some dinner.'

With full tummies, the children happily fall into their beds and dream of the adventures they might come across the next day. Granny Jojo and Rose sit up talking until the small hours; they have over a decade to catch up on!

10

Bucket and Payne

10 August
Sophia

The following day NDA is busy emptying pans of water when the children finally surface. It has bucketed down throughout the night and to NDA's annoyance there is a hole in the caravan roof.

She looks at the children and says, 'That William Payne, giving us a dodgy caravan! I'll have his guts for garters. I've emptied three of these pans out already this morning. These saucepans are just too tiny; you're going to have to find me some bigger buckets from the shower block.'

Sophia looks at NDA with disappointment and says, 'Ahhh, I wanted to go in the sea today.'

Charlie laughs sarcastically, 'Well if Granny stops emptying those pans, you'll be able to swim in here!' He splashes some of the water from the pan into Sophia's face and smirks.

NDA says firmly, 'You two go and get changed. After that you can go on a bucket scavenge.' As the children run out of the door, NDA shouts behind them, 'Don't you forget your anoraks!'

They hear a dodgy rendition of Pharell's Happy coming from the shower block. On the main door there is a sign reading, Cleaning in Progress. Keep Out. The children peek their heads round the door and see site owner William dancing around, using the head of the mop as a microphone. Charlie spies the mop bucket. He turns to Sophia and wickedly whispers, 'I dare you to grab that bucket!'

Sophia, always game for a challenge, rushes in and grabs the bucket. The dirty water spills all over the floor and the two of them burst out laughing. William turns round just in time to see the two of them running out of the door and notices Sophia's long black hair trailing behind her.

Sophia and Charlie run as fast as they can back to NDA's caravan, William chasing frantically behind them with the mop in his hand.

He screams, 'Get back here you two!'

The two children run into the caravan panting and soaking wet. They turn to NDA and proudly hand over the goods.

NDA looks at them both and says, 'About time too!'

Still huffing and puffing, they hear a bang on the door. The two children leg it out of the side door just as William screams, 'Get back here with my bucket, you pair of....'

Before William has a chance to finish his sentence, NDA abruptly opens the door. 'Not you again! You'd better come in. Look at this mess.'

William looks at the bucket and is about to break into a rant when he notices the rainwater streaming through the roof of the caravan. Still catching his breath, he turns to NDA and says, 'Next job on my list, gawgeous! But a cuppa tea wouldn't go amiss!'

Looking at the mop in William's hand, NDA says to him, 'Well, you can mop this floor while you're waiting then!'

William sets to cleaning the floor. As he mops, he thinks to himself, 'I'll deal with those two rascals later.'

After a day of avoiding 'the Payne', Charlie and Sophia are lured back to the caravan by the delicious smell of NDA's baking. They open the door just as she's getting a pie out of the oven.

NDA says, 'Perfect timing!'

They all sit down to dinner and start to munch their way through the tasty food. Then they hear Payne's familiar ratatattat and NDA opens the door.

William says to her, 'I didn't think you'd gone out, so I brought you the site's club timetable. There's bingo and ballroom dancing. You look like you'd be quite nimble on your feet!'

Charlie and Sophia exchange glances. Charlie sticks his fingers in his mouth and pretends to be sick, and Sophia copies him. NDA scowls at them.

Sniffing inquisitively, Payne says, 'Something smells nice!'

Sophia chirps up, 'Yeh, it's NDA's absolutely scrumptious apple pie'.

William hopefully says, 'Ooooh, I'm very partial to a bit of apple pie.'

With that NDA cuts William a large slice of pie and hands it to him. William takes the plate and squeezes in on the bench between Charlie and Sophia. He finishes his pie in two mouthfuls and NDA gets up to make him some tea. While her back's turned, William playfully leans over and takes two scoops out of Charlie and Sophia's bowls. They look at him in shock as he sits there and chuckles. Sophia shouts out,

'Ugh, I don't want any more of that!' and pushes her bowl into the middle of the table.

William leans in and in one fell swoop devours the remainder of Sophia's pudding. NDA looks across and says, 'Ohhh, you two were hungry!'

William walks to the door chuckling and shouts out, 'See you later, gawgeous'.

NDA responds, 'Ooohhh get away with ya!'

Charlie turns to Sophia and says, 'We need to get him back.'

Sophia high fives him, saying, 'This means war!'

11

Mango Tree

24 July
Katie

The children wake to the smell of warm bread. They are so excited to try some of Granny Jojo's cooking. Mum isn't very good at cooking, because she's always in a rush. They had tried yams before but they didn't think much to the taste back at home. Last night, Granny Jojo had promised them a special milkshake made using goats' milk and they couldn't wait!

The children eagerly sit down round the kitchen table and while they are munching happily on Granny Jojo's treats, they hear a noise coming from outside. All the local children are out there playing and calling excitedly to the new visitors. The kitchen door bursts open, the door almost falling off the hinges, and two children rush in. Granny Jojo firmly says, 'Quiet now, calm down, come here and give Granny a kiss. I'd better introduce you to these three musketeers.'

Granny prompts the children sitting at the table, 'Go on, introduce yourselves.'

'Hi, you two, this is Lizzie, she's five….' Katie begins.

Benji butts in,

'I'm Benji, and I'm in charge now that Dad's away!' Katie swats him like a fly and introduces herself,

'And finally, I'm Katie, the oldest,' she says significantly.

Granny continues, 'These are your two terrible twin cousins, Sweetpea and Samuel, known as Sami.'

The twins chant together, 'We're both nine, almost ten!'

They both have a darker skin-tone than their cousins. Sweetpea has her hair in braids and an open smiling friendly face. Sami has a cheeky smile and short-cropped hair. They are both muscular, taller than Benji and Katie, and dressed in light cotton shorts and bright red T-shirts.

Granny calls to the twins, 'Here are your milkshakes, you two.

Drink up and then you can play.'

They greedily gulp down their milkshakes.

Granny Jojo realises there are five children in her kitchen and shoos them all outside, 'Go on all of you, get out and play.'

Immediately, Benji and Sami start a game of One-Two, boys versus girls. Although the children don't know each other, the universal language of football helps them to communicate. In between points, Benji shows off his keepie-uppie skills, trying to beat his latest record.

Granny Jojo finally bursts out of the door, shouting, 'You kids, all out of my yard, shoo with you, shoo!'

Rose comes to the door and Katie runs up to her saying, 'May we go out with them, Mum?'

Rose replies, 'I don't think so darling, I will take you out to explore later.'

Granny Jojo promptly intervenes, 'Let her go, what harm can come to them here? You were always safe, nothing bad ever happened to you!'

Rose inhales sharply, looking shocked that her mother has just interfered. 'Well, take your caps, don't take them off and don't forget your water bottles either.'

Granny Jojo shouts, pointing at Lizzie, 'Forget the water? You've forgotten the baby. Take her with you and have fun! I don't want to see any of you until the sun is high up in that sky.'

As the five of them head out of the gate of the compound the group are joined by other local kids. One of the other children suggests going to play up near the school as there's a playground.

Lizzie starts to get irritable and agitated by the heat, so Katie says, 'Maybe it's best for us to turn back, we're not used to such temperatures.'

Sami suggests, 'Why don't we just head to the river? There are loads of mango trees growing near the water.'

Sweetpea adds, 'Yeah, I can show you where the very best mango trees grow.'

Sami shoots up one of the trees in a matter of seconds and, as the children run to catch up, he's already sitting on the middle branch with a ripe orange mango in his hand.

He shouts down to Benji, 'This isn't a football, this is a mango! Sweetpea will show you how to eat it,' as he throws two more down for Lizzie and Sweetpea.

Sweetpea does a perfect demonstration of how to eat a mango. 'First, you have to hold the mango and squeeze it all the way round to soften the fruit and produce juice. Then you have to peel a small hole in the top of the mango, where you can suck the juice out. Once all the juice has been sucked out you can peel the skin back and eat the flesh.'

Directed at Lizzie, Sweetpea says, 'You will be far more hydrated after drinking this than you would from your bottled water.'

The other children from the village climb the mango tree. Sweetpea thoughtfully takes a mango for Lizzie and starts to prepare it for her, even removing the stone.

Seeing Sami and one of the local boys from the village up the tree, Katie is desperate to join in. Although she is an athletic girl, she has never done any proper climbing before, let alone climbing something without a rope. She makes it easily to the first branch and decides to settle there before tackling the next bit.

Benji shouts up, 'Katie, check those mangoes out on the branches higher up. We'd be able to eat all week off of them! Can you reach?'

Katie nods, thinking to herself, 'There are tons of better fruits higher up, and I can easily get them!' With her newfound confidence, she reaches up, forgetting the golden rule of climbing – three points of contact at all times. As she looks up, Benji shouts out, 'That one there.'

Katie fixes her eyes on the largest, ripest mango she has ever seen and shouts back, 'I've got it!'

Sami and Sweetpea and their friends from the village, Richard and Amber, are all eagerly egging Katie on. They gather round, hands poised ready to catch the best mango of the day. Katie reaches for the next branch, but her flip-flop slips and as she tries to find her footing she clumsily falls to the ground, half-landing on Benji.

All the children roar with laughter like hyenas. Sweetpea rushes over to check Katie is ok. She dusts her off and gives her a sip of water. After the commotion dies down, Katie notices a throbbing pain in her left arm and tells Sweetpea. Sweetpea immediately dips her scarf in the river and then applies an improvised cold compress to the source of the pain. On the way back to the village Sweetpea and Katie chat without stopping. Although the girls are from completely different continents, they are still interested in the same things.

Sweetpea quietly turns to Katie and says, 'Don't worry, I'm always hurting myself as well.'

Katie asks Sweetpea, 'How did you get your hair like that? The beads are beautiful! I wish my hair could look like that.'

Sweetpea replies, 'Yes, I love it. My mum's done it for me specially, as I'm having a party soon. I've got a new red dress as well.' Sweetpea adds, 'If you come back to my house, I'm sure my mum will braid your hair as well.'

Hearing hairdos mentioned Lizzie rushes up, so as not to be forgotten. 'Me too,' she chants, 'me too.'

12

Burying Payne

11 August
Sophia

'What are you two whispering about?' NDA enquires wiggling her nose.

'What? Us, NDA?' Charlie asks.

'Er hum, it's Grandma to you, cheeky,' she smiles, pretending to be cross.

'Nothing really,' Sophia says with her fingers crossed behind her back.

'Why don't I believe you two little scallywags?' NDA replies.

'Grandma, honestly,' Charlie says, 'Scallywags! You sound like something out of a history book!'

'Less of your lip, young man,' NDA says trying to sound stern, but Charlie and Sophia know she is laughing inside. 'You two can carry the bags to the beach,' NDA added, 'I've got plenty of cake and jam sandwiches – your favourite, Sophia!'

'What about me, NDA? I mean, Grandma,' Charlie adds.

'Well I would never forget you, would I? Some cheese straws – your favourite. Oh, and two flasks of tea,' she continues.

'Tea!' Sophia and Charlie shriek.

'Yuk,' the terrible two shout in unison.

'Yes, tea! It's darn hot out there and it will help cool you down,' NDA responds. 'There's no fizzy pop for you two, you're both too hyper as it is!'

'Quite right, my dear Grace,' William beams.

'Oh where did you come from?' NDA had no idea why William, the ever-so-large Payne, was at the door.

'I must say I am very partial to jam sandwiches,' Payne announces.

Sophia and Charlie mimic, 'Ooohh, I am partial to cheese straws.'

'Let me carry these down to the beach for you,' Payne offers

NDA.

'No, no, we'll manage!' Sophia and Charlie protest at the top of their voices.

'Nonsense! These bags are far too valuable to let two pipsqueaks carry, you'll probably drop them!' Payne says sarcastically.

'There won't be enough,' Charlie hisses at Payne.

'Yes, there blooming well will be,' NDA smiles, tucking two more Tupperware boxes full of goodies into the enormous laundry bag. They could have survived all week on the food NDA supplies.

'Come on, Grace,' Payne says chivalrously, helping NDA down the steps of the caravan.

'Wait, you two,' he calls after Sophia and Charlie as they run down to the beach. 'I'll show you the best place to pitch up.'

'Oh, my legs,' NDA grumbles quietly to herself as she walks on the soft sandy beach.

'I'll give you a carry,' Payne says cheekily, winking at NDA.

'Oohh, get away with you,' NDA smiles as she blushes as red as a tomato.

William Payne knows the beach like the back of his hand and he stops at the most beautiful spot next to some beach huts. He takes out his enormous set of keys and walks over to the pale blue beach hut with a pretty white flower painted on the door.

'Here you go, Grace', he says, pulling out a rattan chair that was painted the same baby blue as the beach hut. 'You might like a couple of cushions,' he says, kindly popping down two soft cushions. He then takes out a folded table and three deckchairs. He pulls out a stripy windbreaker to protect NDA from the wind.

With a final flourish, he pulls out a small footstool. NDA is in heaven! William gently lifts up her feet that are wriggling in her bright yellow Crocs.

'Here you go, Grace, you should be nice and comfy now,' he says.

'Ohh, you're spoiling me, Mr Payne,' she giggles, squinting as the sun shines on her soft crumpled face.

'I've got just the thing,' he says and pulls out an orange umbrella with a large black base.

'There, that's better, Grace. Can't have the sun in those lovely blue eyes,' he adds.

'That's very kind,' Grace blushes. Her eyes were a beautiful watery blue.

'Come on!' Charlie shouts back at Sophia as they both run up and down the beach, jumping in the waves as they crash on the shore.

'I wish Vinny were here,' Sophia sighs. This is the longest she's ever been away from Mum, Dad and Vinny, and she is sure they must all be missing her terribly!

After charging around for all of twenty minutes, they both run panting back to NDA and Payne.

'We're starving,' Charlie announces, as he spies NDA's small feast being laid out on Payne's folding table.

'Ermm I'm sure you are,' NDA chuckles – the pair had eaten two rounds of hot buttery toast less than an hour before. 'Come on then, let's all have a nice cup of tea and some homemade scones or fairy cakes,' NDA says putting one of each on Charlie's plate.

Charlie's eyes light up.

'Oh yummy,' Sophia squeals.

NDA is just putting Sophia's treats on a plate when Payne swipes a scone from Charlie and a fairy cake from Sophia. NDA is too busy pouring tea and fussing to notice what is going on.

'Hey, that's not fair,' Sophia shouts, waving a fist at Payne.

'We'll get him back,' Charlie hisses, clenching his teeth.

'Oh lovely, Grace,' Payne smiles, tucking into his fourth scone. 'I've worked up a proper appetite, carrying all this stuff down to the beach.'

'It's only 50 metres,' Sophia points out.

'But you forget I'm a growing lad,' Payne laughs tapping his tummy.

'Lad?!? More like grumpy old fatso,' Charlie whispered to Sophia, just loud enough for Payne to hear.

'I'm full to bursting, thank you NDA,' Sophia says warmly.

'Ahh, it's lovely to be able to see you all having such a nice time.' NDA packs the empty plates in a carrier bag and tucks it under the table. As she sits back down on the soft rattan chair with her feet up on the stool, she soon starts to doze off. Payne's bottom is far too big for the deckchair and he grabs an old pink bathing towel and lays it out on the sand.

'I can't wait for some more of those cheese straws,' he says dreamily into the air and with that he is asleep. Within a few minutes he rolls onto his back, with his head just over to one side.

The sun shines down on him.

'Hey,' Charlie whispers to Sophia, 'Old Payne's asleep! He looks like a beached whale.' Charlie laughs, pointing at Payne, who is now snoring.

'He's so greedy,' Sophia moans. 'It's not fair!'

'Why has he starting hanging around with us?' Charlie grumbles.

'I think he fancies NDA,' Sophia points out.

'Oh my God!' Charlie's face went as white as a sheet. 'That greedy, guzzling gorilla is going nowhere near my gran,' he says protectively. 'It's bad enough my mum's on honeymoon this week. I've just got another dad and I don't want a new granddad! Can you imagine him trying to be my granddad? No blooming way!'

'NDA wouldn't move away, do you think?' Sophia asks worriedly, 'I couldn't bear it. I don't think my dad, mum and Vinny would want to live in a caravan park to be near NDA.' Her bottom lip starts to quiver.

'Come on', Charlie says, 'I've got a plan.'

There are buckets and spades in Payne's beach hut and Charlie had pulled a face when Payne presented him with them earlier.

'Come on Sophia, we've got a lot of work to do,' Charlie says filling one bucket with sand as he starts to cover Payne.

'Oh this is going to take hours,' Sophia grumbles. Just then she spies two large orange buckets outside the beach hut.

'Come on,' Sophia whispers excitedly.

After half an hour in the roasting sun, Charlie and Sophia have covered Payne in half a metre of sand. Only his face is left exposed.

'We've got to make some trenches for the seawater to run into Payne as the tide comes in,' Charlie orders. Sophia carefully copies him, making small ravines in the sand to channel the water from the tide up to Payne's body.

NDA starts to stir and then sits up, rubbing her eyes. 'Oh, you pair,' she laughs quietly, 'I don't know what I'm going to do with you!'

She pours them a cup of tea and they all tuck into the jam sarnies and cheese straws.

'Well at least we don't have to share with poxy Payne,' Charlie hisses.

The tide is starting to come in and the tiny ravines are filling with water. They had made twenty little lakes: some up to his ankles, some to his tummy and a large one up to his neck. Payne is almost completely buried and it looks like there is a large hill of sand on the beach, changing the entire landscape!

'I can't stop laughing,' Sophia roars.

'He's going to get really wet,' Charlie says triumphantly.

As the seawater follows the tiny channels Payne starts to feel a little trickle of cool water around his toes.

'I bet he is dreaming of going for a pee,' Charlie laughs.

'Oohh, I'm not too sure you two. You'd better dig him out; he'll have your guts for garters when he catches you!' NDA exclaims.

Payne starts to stir and tries to stretch.

'Oi, what's happened?' Payne bellows. He opens his eyes to see Sophia and Charlie standing over him.

'You pair of little…' he screams.

'Ha ha!' the pair are laughing uncontrollably.

'Ooh, I'm going to wet myself,' Charlie says, rolling about on the sand. He looks at Sophia and the pair laugh even harder. The tide is now coming in but it is still over ten metres away from Payne.

As Payne wriggles his legs he realises he can free himself easily, but keeps up the pretence that he is trapped to play along with Sophia and Charlie and to gain NDA's sympathy.

'Come on, get me out!' he yells.

NDA says sternly, 'I'm not joking. You need to get him out.' She starts to look worried.

'You two dig me out right now. I'm going to give you both such a good telling off,' Payne shouts, pretending to panic.

'Come on, enough is enough,' NDA says, starting to scoop away the sand.

'But it's not fair,' Sophia whines. 'It's taken us ages to bury him!'

The children start to quickly shovel off the sand. Charlie uses the spade, trying to dig down to Payne's skin.

'Oi!! I felt that,' Payne pipes up as his legs start to get free. Charlie helps to liberate one arm and then shouts to Sophia, 'Quick, leg it!'

'I'll get you two, if it's the last thing I do!' Payne shouts after the pair as they run away.

'Oh, I'm tired,' NDA yawns as she starts walking back to the caravan.

13

Medicine Man

24 July
Katie

In the distance, Rose hears the roar of laughter, getting louder and louder as the children approach. The door flies open and a dusty football lands right in Granny's lap. Benji's small face appears in the doorway, as red as a tomato.

Rose shrieks, 'Benji, how many times have I told you about kicking a football around near a house?'

Granny Jojo interrupts, 'Oh Rose, don't be so harsh on the boy.' She turns to Benji saying, 'If you're not careful this will end up in the pot!' She chest-passes the ball back to him and adds, 'And you, boy, will join it!'

Benji shyly apologises, trying not to look Granny directly in the eye. He doesn't truly know if her threat is real. On the table there are five glasses of Granny's ice-cold lemonade lined up.

Granny addresses the children, 'Now, I want you all to sip this lemonade slowly, none of that gulping from earlier. Let the quench of the lemon get to the back of your throat, you're only allowed one glass!'

Rose stands in the corner looking horrified as she notices the children are covered in sticky mango juice. She shouts at the children, 'What on earth have you done to your new clothes?'

Granny butts in again, 'You know Rose, things have changed around here. We no longer have to take the clothes down to the stream. I've a new machine sitting in the back room. It really doesn't matter that the kids are dirty, they're just clothes.'

Looking furious, Rose firmly orders the children, 'Get upstairs and get changed. No more lemonade till you're in something clean.'

Yet again Granny interrupts, 'Ahh Rose, leave them be, child. They're just going to get dirty again before teatime. You're always fussing around them like a buzzy bee.' Facing the children, Granny orders, 'Sit, drink…and enjoy.'

Rose looks at the kids despairingly and goes to her large bag to find wet wipes. Before all five children know it, Rose is aggressively rubbing any remnants of mango juice from their cheeks.

Granny turns to Rose and says, 'Ahh the pesky fly is back, leave them be.'

Regardless, Rose continues, feeling humiliated in front of her children. She needs some time on her own and heads to the study to email Steve.

To	Steve
From	Rose
Subject	Mum

S,

This place hasn't changed a bit! I can't believe Mum still hasn't painted the kitchen. It's still that lurid yellow, but at least it's faded a bit over the years. Mum's gigantic kitchen table doesn't seem as big as it used to. The benches are still there. Now Mum reigns at the head of the table from Dad's old chair. She's definitely taken Dad's place. I can remember, as children, sitting with Dad in his chair as he recited stories of crocodiles. No one ever sat in Dad's chair without him. It was his. It seems strange seeing Mum sat there.

I'd forgotten how annoying my mum really is. At every turn she's undermining me and she's letting the children run riot. She doesn't get that they're from the UK; they have to have bottled water, they have to have hats, they need to stay clean. The three of them have completely ruined their new clothes, eating mangoes like monsters. They were covered head to toe in mango pulp. There is no chance of me getting them clean. I don't know why I bothered buying them new clothes for this trip!

Mum keeps referring to my children as kids…. They are not baby goats, how dare she?!

> In fact I can hear Mum shouting at me now, and Kai
> and Ivy have just turned up, I can hear his infectious
> laughter coming from the kitchen.

'Come on Rose, lunch is on the table for you, too', Granny Jojo was yelling in the direction of the study.

> Right, better go.
> Hope you're ok and not missing us too much.
> Don't forget the recycling needs to go out tomorrow.
> Love,
> Rose x

Rose comes back to the kitchen to see the whole family sat round the table. The scene is a picture of chaos with kids helping themselves to everything apart from vegetables. Rose can hardly hear herself think, the children are all talking over one another and the adults are no better. The kids' plates are piled with food, mountains of food that they'll never be able to finish.

Rose steps in, saying to Kai, 'Don't give the children so much; they'll waste it. Other children are going hungry!'

Granny butts in, 'There's no one going hungry in this house! This is one of the first decent meals these children have eaten.'

Rose has to stop herself and count to ten. She looks at the others and everyone is having fun. She thinks to herself, 'Why is it I feel like an outsider in my own family?'

She watches the children eating with their hands; it's like feeding time at the zoo. She suddenly notices the white scarf wrapped around Katie's forearm and shouts, 'Katie, what's happened to your arm?!'

Silence falls over the table and everyone turns to face Rose. Rose repeats, 'What on earth have you done to your arm?'

Before Katie has a chance to answer, Sami and Benji pipe up, 'She fell out of the mango tree, ha ha.' They jump up to re-enact the scene for everyone. Sami stands on the kitchen bench and encourages Benji to climb up and put his feet in his hands. Benji is now 1.5m in the air and he dramatically throws himself down, mimicking Katie's fall. The pair shout out in unison, 'OW OW OW!'

The kids are all hyperactive and uncontrollable, thanks to all the sugary treats that Granny Jojo has filled them with. Uncle Kai is sat in the corner encouraging all the theatrics, while Granny Jojo sits there tutting.

Before Rose can inspect Katie's injury, Ivy quickly unties the bandage. She stands up and says, 'I'll go and get a potion from the medicine man!'

'Great idea, Ivy,' Granny Jojo responds. 'Tell him I'll sort out the money with him.'

Before Rose has a chance to even question the treatment, Ivy floats out of the back door with her scarf billowing behind her.

Rose cradles Katie like a baby and takes her into the sitting room. The sitting room walls are covered from floor to ceiling in wood panelling, and there is a strong smell of furniture polish. The overpowering smell of polish evokes such strong memories in Rose. As children they were never allowed to play in the sitting room – they were only allowed in there for high-days and holidays.

Rose sits on the sofa with Katie on her lap. The sun is streaming through the window, covering them both in brilliant light. She examines Katie's arm. Rose realises that it isn't broken and she is relieved to see Katie moving all her fingers.

'What on earth were you thinking? You're supposed to be the sensible one! You've been out here less than 24 hours and already you're jeopardising the holiday,' Rose snaps.

Katie bursts into tears, more from relief than pain. She blubbers, 'Mum, I'm sorry. I just wanted to be like the others. I didn't mean to slip.'

Seeing Katie upset, Rose turns to her and gives her a massive kiss.

'It's all right darling, we'll get you fixed up and then we'll both enjoy the rest of the holiday.'

Without Rose and Katie realising it, Ivy has appeared in the room with the healer. Katie and Rose look up to see a tall, black shadow, and the temperature in the room instantly drops. Katie feels a shiver race up her spine and clings desperately to Rose. The healer takes his stick with a horsetail and waves it frantically around the room, mumbling. Granny Jojo appears with a handful of notes to pay the healer and he starts flicking water around to purify the room.

The healer approaches Katie, sitting on Rose's lap. Rose

immediately turns her back to the healer to protect Katie, shouting, 'Enough is enough! I'm not allowing any of this hocus-pocus to be performed on my daughter. Get him out of here now!'

The healer shrugs, leaves an iridescent blue feather on the coffee table for Katie and walks out. Katie looks up to see the healer leaving and he smiles broadly at her. Ivy drifts out with him.

Granny Jojo turns to Rose and says, 'Why the fuss? No harm ever came to you!'

Rose stands up and walks stiffly out of the room. Granny Jojo follows quickly after her.

Katie, intrigued by recent events, leans down and picks up the shiny blue feather. She gently brushes it on her skin and is fascinated by the sensation.

To	Steve
From	Rose
Subject	Mum

Steve

How are things at home?

I'm struggling out here.

Mum is so stuck in the past and Ivy encourages all her nonsense. I can't begin to tell you how superstitious they are.

The children have settled in.

Katie has been climbing a tree, she fell out, more hurt pride, I think, than anything else.

Don't forget that hole in the fence still needs repairing since Benji kicked a ball straight through it.

Rose x

Granny Jojo comes into the study with two glasses of milk for them.

'Why are you so stressed child, what's the matter with you? You never used to be so uptight. Look what the West has done to you. You have the whole world on your shoulders, bringing up those three children. You've been so blessed with such beautiful children. I see so much of you in Katie. And now look at you! You look like you're sucking on a lemon the whole time. What was all the commotion about earlier? The child just had a little knock. You can't wrap them up in cotton wool the whole time! You embarrassed me in front of the good healer.'

Frustrated, Rose leans across and says, 'The children have been brought up with manners, respect and firm boundaries, and you're undoing all our hard work. You're undermining everything Steve and I believe to be right. I can't understand why you still believe in all this hocus-pocus nonsense. Did you actually think his feather and water could help her?'

Granny Jojo retorts, 'You think your Western medicine has all the answers? You think you're better than us now you're practising in your Western hospital? I raised all you children single-handed; no harm came to any of you.'

Through clenched teeth Rose spits, 'So what happened to Daisy then?'

Granny replies, 'Daisy was a child; she got an infection. When I carried her back from the forest how could anyone know she'd be taken so ill? I grieve every day for that child. How dare you say her name so thoughtlessly? That child was our treasure. She was my first-born and will always have the dearest part of my heart.

Rose spits, 'They were twins!'

Granny Jojo replies, 'I've said too much. I'm going to bed. I hope you wake in the morning with some joy in your heart and remember where you are. Don't forget you are back in Africa!'

14

The Pleasure Beach Fiasco

11 August 6.30pm
Sophia

'Oh NDA,' Charlie whines, 'why do you have to go?'

'Oh Charlie, I'm sure you and Sophia can entertain yourselves for one evening!' NDA reasons, ruffling her grandson's hair affectionately.

'But bingo and dancing, with Payne,' Charlie protests.

'Oh, he's not so bad and, look, he's left us this big book of vouchers. It's just a bit of adult company for me,' NDA says gently.

'Are we not enough for you?' Sophia looks into NDA's blue eyes.

'My Gawd! You are more than enough for anyone. If you really don't want me to go, then I'll stay,' NDA says sincerely. 'Look, Mr Payne also left all these board games for you and he's left his deluxe Scrabble.'

'I hate ruddy Scrabble, it's for swots!' complains Sophia.

'So it's got nothing to do with the fact you can't spell, dear?' NDA says, teasing.

'Even if I could spell, I'd hate it,' Charlie jumps in.

'Yeah, it's like ruddy homework disguised as a game. I hate it when Vinny, the nerdy swot, gets it out at home,' Sophia says with her eyes welling up, as if she is about to cry.

Charlie is looking through Payne's voucher books when he suddenly pipes up as bright as a button, 'Listen NDA, you go and have a good time. Sophia and I can look after ourselves.' Charlie sounds very grown up.

'Really, you sure son?' NDA smiles as she quickly pulls on her beautiful blue and silver shawl that Jasmine had bought her last Christmas. As she rushes out of the door, clutching a large Tupperware box containing fairy cakes and cheese straws, she passes the box to Sophia and says, 'Look, there are plenty of treats in here and you've both had your tea already. No one will starve in this caravan!'

Charlie cheekily shouts after her, 'Don't do anything we wouldn't do!'

As NDA disappears towards the clubhouse Sophia says, 'What do you think you're doing? She's spending the night with our sworn enemy, you blooming pillock!'

'Forget them,' Charlie says, smiling.

He hands Sophia a voucher and says, 'Look what I've found in Payne's voucher pile.'

'Oh my god,' Sophia squeals with delight. 'Two free passes to the adventure theme park! Do you think we dare? NDA said she wouldn't let us go, because there are too many big kids there.'

'Blooming heck, Sophia, she's going to be out for ruddy hours with that porky Payne,' Charlie replies.

'Okay, give me a minute. I want to put on my new jeans,' Sophia says, rushing into the other room.

Within seconds the two are running as fast as they can towards the pleasure beach. As they approach the turnstile, Sophia comes to a halt.

'No children under 16 unaccompanied by an adult,' she pants.

'Oh, what are we going to do now?' Charlie whines. 'We'll never pass for 16.'

There is a small queue of parents and their children at the kiosk. They both look at each other as another family approach. They wait until the family has almost passed through the entrance and then run up behind with Sophia shouting, 'We can hand in our own vouchers, Aunty Jane.'

The mother of the group looks around, understandably confused. Sophia hands the two vouchers to the smiley lady at the turnstile,

'We're with them,' Sophia smiles sweetly pointing to the strange new adopted family ahead of her. Aunty Jane and...'

Charlie pokes Sophia in the back, not wanting her to get too carried away with her acting. The lady on the turnstile gives both Charlie and Sophia access-all-area wristbands and says, 'Your aunt's got the map.'

With that, they are in!

Charlie couldn't believe it. 'Wow Sophia! That was ingenious. You're not half bad for a girl,' he adds.

Sophia beams with pride.

As dusk approaches the lights shine even more brightly from the funfair and the music appears to get even louder. Sophia and Charlie run excitedly from ride to ride. Charlie searches his pockets and produces some more vouchers:

Dunky Doughnuts – 10 free on the production of this voucher.

'Cool, I love funfair doughnuts! I had some last summer with Mum, Dad and Vinny,' Sophia exclaims, as a pang of sadness overwhelms her. She is really starting to miss everyone at home now.

'Come on, we've got four vouchers, so that's 20 each,' Charlie calls out to her. He grabs hold of Sophia's arm and drags her over to the doughnut stand. Sophia manages a substantial 10 doughnuts, but the award for top doughnut munching goes to Charlie as he ploughs through an impressive 30! They both decide to wait for ten minutes until all the doughnuts have been digested, before attempting the high-top ride.

Unbeknown to Sophia and Charlie, at the bingo NDA is winning prizes left, right and centre. She's already won rose talc, a bottle of bubbly and two tickets to the Pleasure Beach! All the other residents at the caravan park are very disgruntled, as NDA does the supermarket sweep on all the bingo prizes. William Payne surely hasn't stitched up the competition?! NDA is by far the most excited about the Pleasure Beach tickets and can't wait to tell Sophia and Charlie.

'Ohhhhh, my Charlie and Sophia will be so-oo excited! They've been pestering me all week to go to that Pleasure Beach,' NDA says excitedly. 'Maybe we could all go tomorrow? You wouldn't mind running us all up in your car would you?' She says looking pleadingly at William Payne.

'It would be a pleasure, my dear, to take you to the Pleasure Beach,' William Payne smarmily answers.

NDA says, 'I think I ought to check in on those two rascals before we do anything else.'

'Take my arm, Grace, I'll walk you back,' William says.

NDA's maternal alarm is immediately sounded when she spots that all the lights are off in the caravan. She turns to William and worriedly says, 'Something's not right, where are they?'

Looking round the caravan William notices the remains of his voucher book scattered over the table. He turns to Grace and says, 'I know just where they are. You wait here, Grace, I'll go and collect them in my car.'

Charlie feels really quite peculiar. Maybe 35 doughnuts were a bit excessive? They do one loop on the high-top ride before being greeted again by those 30 sugar-coated round treats. Charlie's poorly digested doughnuts cover everyone on the ride!

Sophia says, 'Oh my goddddd, you've covered everyone in puke! I'm proper glad I was sat next to you. Thankfully, you've failed to spray me!'

As the ride jolts to a stop, Sophia looks at Charlie with his sickly, slimy, stinky face and the gross globules covering his T–shirt. She thinks to herself, 'We're in trouble.'

She quickly raises the safety harness and jumps up. Suddenly a big black shadow falls over the pair of them. Sophia shouts out, 'PAYNE!'

And, on cue, Charlie projectile pukes all down Payne's perfectly pressed penguin suit – his pride and joy worn for the bingo hall.

'URGHHHHHHH!' Payne screams out. He is completely splattered by Charlie's vile vomit.

Sophia is already legging it towards the gate as Payne calls out, 'Get back here, girl. I'm taking you both back to Grace.'

Charlie starts whimpering and Payne scoops him up and carries him to the back of the truck. Payne felt pangs of sympathy for poor little Charlie, but there was no way someone in his state would make it into the cab part of the truck.

Payne says, 'You're not getting any more of your putrid puke over my truck or me. You're riding out back in the pick–up. It'd take me a week to get the smell of sick out of the upholstery!'

Sophia can't leave Charlie, so she sheepishly joins Payne in the cab of the truck.

When the three of them arrive back at the campsite, NDA is standing in the doorway, already getting whiffs of vile vomit. Payne stops the truck, hauls little Charlie out of the pick-up and presents him to NDA.

Sophia calls out, 'Charlie's been a bit unwell. Don't be cross, NDA. It wasn't the fair that made him sick, I think he ate a bad doughnut.'

'Well that's blooming obvious! You better get straight in that shower – WITH your clothes on,' NDA calls out angrily.

15

Spiders and Snakes

11 August
Katie and Benji visit their cousins' house

Benji hated getting up at home; it was a constant battle. Katie always got up early, and her clothes would be neatly hanging on a satin hanger on her wardrobe door.

Benji's football shirt and shorts would be in a pile on the floor next to him all crumpled and creased.

Rose would do the 'I'm counting to 5' routine and normally at 4 and ¾ Benji would run into the bathroom, grabbing his tablet on the way so that he could play a quick game of football. Meanwhile the queue outside the bathroom grew longer and Benji ended up not leaving himself time to brush his teeth properly.

Katie was too smart for him. She always got into the bathroom early, because she had been caught out in the past, banging on the door waiting for Benji to finish a game or a comic he had hidden in there. However on holiday it was different. The sun forced its way through the wooden shutters into his bedroom, making it impossible to go back to sleep.

Benji is staying in the room Uncle Kai had as a boy, and not too much had changed. Out of the window the old rope ladder was still there and Benji awakes to see Sami tapping on the shutter as he hung with one arm on the rope. Benji opens the shutter and Sami falls into the room. Both boys laugh uncontrollably as Sami lands in Benji's suitcase. All Benji's sweets go flying and so did his magic tricks.

Sami screams when he sees the spider and snake. Benji falls out of bed laughing at the joke and with that, the boys are best of friends.

Sami and Benji climb down the rope ladder intent on mischief, both carrying some jelly worms and a fake snake and spider.

Katie hears the commotion and sees Benji and Sami disappear

next door. She carefully slides down the rope ladder, being careful not to hurt her arm.

Sami and Sweetpea share a bedroom with a wall made out of a curtain drawn across the room to divide it in half. Kai had offered to make a solid wall but for now the twins enjoyed sharing a room.

Benji and Sami are plotting how to scare everyone with Benji's case of tricks. As Sweetpea puts her head around the curtain she sees both boys with their jelly worms hanging out of their mouths.

'Ahhh', she screams as both boys suck the sweets making Sweetpea shriek even louder. At that point Katie appears and snatches a handful of Benji's sweet jelly worms and shares the joke with Sweetpea.

'That's disgusting! I thought they were real and worms that colour must be poisonous!'

Both boys carry on laughing and can see how this would scare Granny Jojo and plan to trick her too as soon as they can. Benji and Sami decide to take more sweets out to scare the other children and anyone else they can find. The sugary jellies are making Sami very excitable.

Katie and Sweetpea decide to spend the day playing on the iPad. They take photos of each other and then add different makeup styles and add extra-long lashes and change their hair colour. Sweetpea is fascinated as she has never used the app before.

'If you like that, you'll love this one!', smiles Katie, opening up another app.

The new app allows you to lip-sync to music, and the girls spend ages practising different dance routines and then lip-sync to Sweetpea's favourite song.

At first Sami is impressed when he sees the downloaded video but eight views later he can't pretend to be interested anymore.

The boys are bored and go off to plant the spider and snake in Granny Jojo's bedroom.

'I know, let's put one of your giant spiders in Granny Jojo's slipper and a snake in her big sugar tub', Sami suggests excitedly. The boys start hiding their tricks.

Within minutes they hear Granny Jojo scream.

'Ha ha', they laugh, 'Got her!' The boys high-five.

Hearing their laughter she shouts, 'I'll get you two!'

The boys run out into the yard laughing and screaming.

As Granny Jojo calms down, the girls show her the pictures on the tablet of the different makeup looks they have created.

'You girls grow up so fast', she smiles.

Ivy appears and snatches the iPad.

'What do you think you are doing? Wearing makeup? Shame on you!'

'I haven't really, Mummy', Sweatpea tried to convince her mother.

'It's just an app on the iPad, Aunty Ivy…' Katie begins.

'You're grounded Sweetpea! You'll bring disgrace on this family; all made up like a cheap tramp. Enough! Go to your room and no supper tonight for you either, you wicked girl'.

With that Ivy and her white scarf wafts away.

Katie is shocked.

'Granny Jojo, that's not fair. We never put makeup on. It was just a programme on my tablet – a game. Aunty Ivy doesn't understand'.

Katie bursts into tears, hating the fact she has got her cousin and now her best friend into trouble.

Granny Jojo replies weakly, 'You know your Granny would never interfere when Ivy gets mad'.

Katie can't stop thinking about Sweetpea and when it is dark she grabs a handful of Benji's chocolate and carefully slips down the rope ladder. She throws some small pebbles up towards Sweetpea's bedroom window.

A red-faced Sweetpea peers down.

'Can you let me in?' Katie whispers up.

'I'm not allowed downstairs', Sweetpea sniffs.

'Have you got anything I can climb up?' Katie insists. 'I've got some chocolate for you, you must be starving.'

Sweetpea hurriedly looks around the room and finally decides to take down her curtain wall to use as a rope for Katie to climb up. Hanging the curtain out of the window, Sweetpea ties the other end to her bed.

Katie gingerly starts to climb up trying to hold onto the chocolate, which is now starting to melt in her hot palms.

Centimetre by centimetre she climbs and when she is almost halfway up, the curtain starts to come undone where it is tied around the bed.

Sweetpea grabs hold of that end too. 'Get a move on Katie!', she whispers through gritted teeth as she feels her friend's weight on the curtain.

At last Katie is through the window and tumbles in a heap on the floor.

'I'm so sorry Sweetpea', Katie says, still out of breath from her climb.

'I had no idea your mum would be so angry and wouldn't believe us', Katie explains.

'It's not your fault Katie', Sweetpea says generously. 'My mum wouldn't believe us about the app now even if you showed her. She's very strict. You'd better go. If she finds you up here I have no idea what she'll do.'

Sweetpea hurriedly eats all the sticky and slimy chocolate.

Katie is dreading the climb down. She decides to go halfway and then jumps the rest of the way, landing in a heap on the ground.

16

BBQ

12 August
Katie

Uncle Kai and Ivy's house is just next-door, but feels a million miles away because it's so modern. There is marble throughout the hall and kitchen and Ivy's influence in the design is obvious, as everything is as white as her trusted shawl. It's a simple bungalow with a roof terrace where Ivy can hang all the washing out to dry. There are palm trees at the end of the garden but a patio covers the rest of the land. Uncle Kai sees himself as a barbeque king and he has a massive grill and bar with several loungers dotted around for people to relax on.

Today, Kai has decided to host a barbeque for his whole family. In fact, he's already preparing the meat for later. The smell of fragrant chicken wafts over the wall into Granny's garden and acts as an invite for them all to come round.

Granny sucks her teeth as she lifts her tired body up off the chair.

'Why the boy didn't put a hole in the fence so I could walk straight through to his yard, I don't know! These young people with their new-fangled ideas…' Granny Jojo exclaims.

As Granny enters Kai's back garden, she says, 'Now you don't expect me to sit on that thing do ya?'

Kai quickly responds, 'Course not, Mumma!'

He effortlessly vaults over the 6ft wooden fence and then dangles Jojo's favourite chair over and calls the boys to help. 'Sami, Benji, come and get this.'

He passes the chair to the boys and then vaults back over as effortlessly as he had done before. Kai positions the chair near the barbeque and picks up his mother, saying, 'There you go Mumma, your throne awaits!'

Kai places Granny Jojo in her chair and she nods her head regally, taking on her role of queen of the family. Rose looks over and laughs, 'Ha ha, careful, Kai, will you never grow up?'

Kai retorts, 'I really hope not, Sis!'

He immediately turns up the music and grabs Ivy's hand for a dance. As Ivy spins, her white silk scarf floats behind her like a translucent tail. The children all join in and spin each other round.

Kai turns to his mother, 'Now Mumma, you gonna give your favourite son a dance tonight?'

'Ah Kai,' Granny Jojo responds, 'You don't want to be dancing with an old lady like me!'

She gets to her feet, picks up Lizzie and pretends to do the waltz. Katie rushes over to the pair and gives Granny Jojo a hug. Granny Jojo gently raises Katie's chin with her hand so she can see clearly into Katie's eyes. She asks, 'Is the arm OK now, child?'

Rose sees the intimacy between the three of them and her heart melts. Rose's foot even starts tapping to the music. She soon loosens up and shouts over to Kai, 'Hey, where's my dance?!' Both stand up and casually dance.

'I've got a surprise for you all. We're all going on a mystery trip on Friday!' Kai whispers in her ear.

Rose asks, 'What trip? When? Where?'

'When you hear me beeping the horn outside the house, that's when. Where, you'll find out when we get there. Why, because it's going to be fun!' Kai whispers back.

In that instant Kai raises Rose off the ground and spins her round, feet off the ground. When the dance finishes, Kai runs over to the barbeque, grabs a chicken leg and throws it in Rose's direction, shouting, 'Ro, catch!'

To everyone's surprise, Rose catches the chicken leg and starts gnawing at the bone.

'Cheers Kai, delicious!' Rose responds.

The house is suddenly filled with family from all over. All four of Kai and Rose's sisters along with their husbands and swarms of children enter the back garden. They are all carrying massive bowls of food, which completely cover the table. This is the first time the whole family has been together in 15 years. Along with the family, all the friends from the village come to celebrate as well.

Granny Jojo puts her arms out, and gathers all the grandchildren towards her and proudly, with a tear in her eye, says, 'All my babies, all home at once, all returned to me, all my babies, all safe.'

To Katie, Granny Jojo says, 'Go to the kitchen, get the dish from the side and bring it to me.'

Turning to Rose, Granny Jojo says, 'You think I'd forget your favourite? Banana dipped in chocolate sauce!'

Granny Jojo puts her hand up for a high-five and Rose responds, 'Nah nah Mumma, high ten!' and shows Granny Jojo both her palms.

At this point the whole party erupts into a high-five, low-five, side-five frenzy, culminating in the whole family falling into fits of giggles! Katie asks Rose for Dad's camera. Rose agrees and Katie runs into the house to collect it, completely forgetting the choco-bananas. Once she's back outside she sets the self-timer to take a photo of the whole family.

Katie shouts out, 'Say cheese!'

Rose butts in, 'No, yam!'

And with that, everyone shouts out 'yam' for the photo. This photo will turn out to be one of Katie's favourite photos from the whole trip. Katie rushes back in to get the choco-bananas. They are soon passed round and Benji, Katie and Lizzie show everyone how to make choco-banana smiles. Benji takes to the stage telling everyone to cut the banana in half and then cut it into 5cm chunks. Everyone is then ordered to place the banana in his or her mouth and pull the biggest grin possible. Some of the smiles are white thanks to the banana flesh, while others are black, due to the chocolate covering! Even Granny Jojo joins in.

Katie brings the camera out again to capture the moment.

Granny Jojo proudly exclaims, 'All my babies together,' struggling to hold back the tears.

Just as the photo is being taken, Rose turns to her older sister Lily and says, 'Well, all of Mum's babies aren't actually here, are they? What about Daisy?'

A look of horror passes over Lily's face. Rose has never mentioned Daisy before. She pulls her to one side and says, 'Let's talk about this somewhere quieter.'

Granny Jojo, unaware of the conversation between the two sisters, calls over to Lily and says, 'Run and fetch the punch bowl, darling.'

Lily looks over at Granny Jojo and nods. Katie thinks to herself, 'I can see where Mum gets it from; Granny Jojo is forever getting people to fetch and carry for her. Not the Jojo gene but the do-do gene – do this, do that, don't do this, don't do that. I hope I don't end up being a do-doer!'

Just as Katie is thinking this, Granny Jojo calls over to Katie, 'Go and get some lemonade for the young'uns, kid'.

Rose and Lily head off to Granny's kitchen. Lily is the spitting image of Jojo and, over time, she has even adopted a lot of her mannerisms.

Katie is a few seconds behind her mum and aunty, and as she reaches the hallway she hears, 'Why are you digging up the past? You've not been here for 15 years and now you're trying to bring up things you will never understand. Why are you the one who always spoils everything? Can't you see how happy Mumma is with all of us around?'

Rose answers, 'Well no, we're not all here, that's the point! I need to understand what happened to Daisy. Mumma said she died from an infection when she brought her back from the forest. What happened?'

Lily quickly answers, 'We were just children. That all happened a long time ago. Let the past be the past! So, how many days are you here for? You're going back to your nice cosy life soon and I'm not picking up the pieces once you're gone!'

Katie can feel her heart beating as she stands there listening to the conversation. She tries to make herself as invisible as possible. She tries to hold her breath to minimise any noise; the only sound is her heart thumping. She closes her eyes to concentrate on what is being said.

Rose replies, 'All I want to do is understand. You've always been so strong. You were always the one I could turn to. You are the only one who properly knew Daisy; I was only two when she died. And now Mumma says she died from an infection. What happened out there in the forest? Did wild animals attack her? Mumma said she brought you both back. What were you and Daisy doing out in the forest? Mumma wouldn't leave you there.'

Lily says, 'You forget I was still a child. I was the one who lay there next to Daisy waiting for Mumma to come and collect us. I was the one who had to watch Daisy slip away.'

Katie felt sick. Her legs were trembling uncontrollably. She wanted to scream, but knew the others would hear her. Millions of thoughts were dashing through her mind:

'Who was Daisy?

How had she died?

Was she part of some ritualistic sacrifice?
Did wild animals kill her?
Why were the two young children left in the forest alone?
Were they my age?
Why couldn't they just run back home?'

Katie is overcome with anxiety and feels all sweaty and clammy. She feels a cold chill envelope her. A shiver runs from the top of her spine to the bottom. A tall dark shadow descends on her. Katie catches a glimpse of Ivy's scarf as it engulfs her. Before Katie knows it, she's back at the barbeque.

17

Freedom Song Talent Contest

13 August
Sophia

'But it's not fair – rain, rain, rain. This is so-ooo boring, can't we go out?' Sophia calls out.

'I'm starting to feel claustrophobic in this tin can,' Charlie says, as he punches the flimsy caravan wall.

'Stop that! I don't know how we'd explain the dented walls to Mr Payne! And he's been so good to us,' NDA replies affectionately. 'I haven't seen Mr Payne since puke-gate,' NDA adds.

'What?!' Sophia asks.

'Don't worry, that's NDA trying to be clever, adding the word gate to any event that goes wrong,' Charlie says.

Sophia thinks to herself, 'I don't truly know what he's going on about, but I'll just smile.'

'Come on, you've got lots to be getting on with! When you spoke to Vinny on the phone yesterday, she gave you lots of competition ideas to be getting on with,' NDA says to Sophia.

'Yeah, Sophia! I thought you said we were going to win all these prizes. Instead we're sat, cramped in this crappy caravan – with the occasional Payne!' Charlie sneers.

'Well, there is one that we could try. You know I'm a fantastic singer, Charlie?' Sophia says.

'Oh my gawdd', NDA mutters.

'I'm planning to win X-Factor. I'm just waiting for them to bring the age group down so I can enter,' Sophia says proudly. Sophia treats them to a rendition of her high-pitched operatic screech, as Charlie sticks his fingers in his ears and pokes his tongue out.

'Yeah, so there is the Write a Song competition for Freedom Charity. They need someone to write and perform a song. They have two iPads to give away to the winners,' Sophia informs him.

Charlie's ears prick up at the possibility of winning a new iPad. He's ended up with his mum's old iPad and all the apps were *running so slowly on it. He's had his eye on a new iPad for months.*

'Hmmm, maybe. It might just be worth it,' he answers. 'I thought it was a bit naff entering all these competitions but if the prize is that good, and we can enter together, it might be a goer,' he adds.

With that he scours through the small print to check there are definitely two iPads up for grabs.

'Amazing! I can't wait to get a white one. What colour would you want? Do you reckon they'll give us a special cover? I can't wait to take it to school. My friend Katie uses hers all the time. Her case has a keyboard attached to it, but I think I'd rather just tap on the screen. Mum and Dad have known for ages that I need an iPad,' Sophia continues.

'Need or want?' NDA asks Sophia pointedly.

Charlie and Sophia are so wrapped up in the thought of winning an iPad that they don't notice Payne's ratatattat at the door.

'Oooh my, don't you look like a scrumptious crumpet?!' Payne smarmily calls to NDA.

'Don't be sooo saucy!' NDA blushes back at him.

Charlie puts his fingers in his ears and almost pretends to puke, until he remembers puke-gate from the other day! Payne whisks NDA off for a champagne afternoon tea in the local hotel. Even after the puke-gate mishap NDA is too loved up and flattered to worry about leaving them. As she rushes out of the door she leaves the pair with a tray of cheese toasties and two mugs of hot chocolate. Sophia is so absorbed in her scale warm-ups that she doesn't notice NDA and Payne leaving together.

Charlie turns to Sophia and says, 'We need to get cracking. The competition closes in two days! It's been running for the last five weeks, Sophia. We could have started this much earlier!'

Sophia larks around, simultaneously singing her scales and pretending to pirouette. Charlie pulls out his old battered iPad with the cracked screen and immediately pulls up the Freedom Charity website (www.freedomcharity.org.uk). He hurriedly starts scribbling down lyrics and calls out to Sophia, 'Come on Sophia, I need you to sit down and concentrate! I need you to search for useful words.'

After hours of beavering away, Sophia and Charlie finally come up with a list of useful words and phrases.

Sophia's list:

- *Freedom;*
- *Freedom to choose;*
- *Freedom to follow your dreams.*

Charlie's list:

- *A time to grow;*
- *A time to know your own mind;*
- *Choose the life you live;*
- *Reach for the skies and open your eyes.*

To Sophia's amazement Charlie starts playing tunes on his keyboard app. He asks Sophia to sing the various lyrics in time with his melody. At that instant a slightly tipsy and red-faced NDA walks through the caravan door. Sophia is mid-song and continues singing, 'Freee-dom, freee-dom.'

NDA joins in and repeats the chorus with Sophia adding the final magic touch:

'Freee-dom, freee-dom, oh oh oh oh
Freee-dom, Freee-dom, oh oh oh oh.'

The three of them go to sleep with the song running through their minds, and the following morning NDA is still 'oh oh oh oh oh'ing away. Charlie looks over in despair seeing Payne tucking into a fry-up.

Payne says to Charlie, 'Ohhhh, I'm partial to a dippy egg,' as he hands his plate up to NDA for more.

Charlie sneers questioningly, 'Seconds? Or is that thirds?'

Sophia and NDA loudly serenade the others in unison, as Payne pipes in, 'I've entered you two in the weekly caravan talent competition! It's in the main hall at 8pm.'

He leans over to Charlie for a high five, but Charlie just blanks him. Payne adds, 'I'll make sure I've got my camcorder on to film you both.'

Sophia squeals with delight and continues dancing round the caravan. Payne sarcastically whispers to Charlie, 'I'm sure it'll make great outtake-TV!'

After breakfast, Charlie and Sophia head straight to the main hall to practise. Charlie is concerned about playing on a proper piano; he'd only ever played on his iPad app. The pair of them don't even come back for tea! Unaware of the hall filling up with spectators, Charlie and Sophia continue practising. In order to fill the hall to capacity, Payne has extended happy hour to last all evening. Every resident is sat there and Payne has even poached caravanners from the neighbouring site.

NDA coos, 'Such a huge crowd! Oooh, Willie, you've done so well.'

William Payne flushes at the flattery. Various talented holidaymakers perform, from spoon-players to jugglers, toothless-granddad-rappers to ballroom dancers. Payne has deliberately scheduled Sophia and Charlie to be the final act and to everybody's amazement the pair end up stealing the show. Charlie's delicate and determined fingers dance all over the piano keys. His floppy blond hair bobs along in time to the music. Sophia stands centre stage with an old-style microphone in front of her. She feels like a 1950s superstar as the stage lighting circles her. Although she feels like a celebrity, she is overcome with anxiety, her palms are sweating and her heart is in her mouth. She thinks to herself, 'I can't let Charlie down, but I wish I could just run and hide.'

She opens her mouth and quietly sings the first line. The audience claps encouragingly, giving Sophia confidence to stand up straighter and project her voice. She gives an awesome performance, as NDA joins her stage left to sing the 'oh oh oh oh oh's in unison. Many of the audience rise to their feet, holding up an array of lighters and drinks as well as phones to video the performance.

As the song crescendos to an end, Sophia and Charlie are met with a standing ovation. Payne, who had been filming the whole performance, swings the camera round to capture the audience's rapturous response. Sophia runs over to Charlie, takes his hand and the pair bow repeatedly with Sophia blowing exaggerated kisses out to their adoring audience. NDA pulls them both to her and affectionately kisses them on the head. Payne presents them both with first prize – two inclusive tickets to the Pleasure Beach. He ruffles Charlie's hair fondly and says, 'Dunky-doughnut vouchers not included!'

18

Safari

16 August
Katie

BEEP BEEP, BEEEP BEEEEEEEP BEEEP BEEEP
BEEP BEEP, BEEEP BEEEEEEEP BEEEP BEEEP
BEEP BEEP, BEEEP BEEEEEEEP BEEEP BEEEP
BEEP BEEP, BEEEP BEEEEEEEP BEEEP BEEEP

That was the tantalising summons. Everyone has been waiting with trepidation.

'Enough, enough!' Granny Jojo is shouting. 'Quiet Kai, you'll give me a headache!'

The twins rush in through the front door making the same racket as their father. They are screaming, 'Benji, Katie, Lizzie, get moving. We want to hit the road!'

The house is filled with chaos, commotion and carnage as everyone gathers their things for the trip. Granny Jojo is secretly fuelling the frenzy, giving all the kids sweets from the counter. Mass hysteria covers the house. Rose slowly walks down the stairs carrying all the children's bags. She shakes her head and says, 'Is this worth it?'

Granny Jojo looks up and jokes, 'Let your hair down darling!'

Lily sarcastically chips in, 'You might even have some fun!'

Rose shakes her head as the beeping continues and takes the bags out to the minibus. Everyone piles into the bus except Granny Jojo, Lily and Ivy who are staying at home. Rose has one last look back and all she sees is Granny Jojo and Lily mysteriously disappearing under Ivy's white scarf.

Granny Jojo looks at the clock in the hallway and says, 'Ay Ay Ay! It's only five o'clock, I think I'm going to take my weary body back to bed for an hour!'

Rose shouts to Kai, 'You're not driving anywhere until all these children have got their seatbelts on!'

Kai nods and laughs, 'OK, Sis. Seatbelts on, kids!'

Kai leans forward and places a CD in the drive. Suddenly Hakuna Matata blasts out over the speakers. The kids all immediately start singing and Rose can't help but laugh. She had sent this CD out for the twin's birthday. It had been their favourite ever since.

Hakuna Matata!
What a wonderful phrase
Hakuna Matata!
Ain't no passing craze
It means no worries for the rest of your days
It's our problem-free philosophy
Hakuna Matata! Hakuna Matata! Hakuna matata!
Hakuna Matata! Hakuna matata! Hakuna Matata!
Hakuna matata! Hakuna Matata! Hakuna matata!

Three hours later they drive through the gates of a safari park, and everyone realises what the surprise will be – SAFARI!

Katie freezes. Terror engulfs her face and her whole body trembles. She thinks to herself, are we going to be left out in the forest like Aunty Daisy?

Kai pulls in. He throws each of them a safari hat and says to Rose, 'Come on, you too!'

All the children except Katie are bursting with excitement, desperate to get going. A tall, strong man appears and he and Kai embrace warmly. Kai introduces the family to Henry, their guide for the day. Directed at Henry, Kai says laughingly, 'I don't want any of my brood ending up as dinner!'

Henry smiles reassuringly and pats his ranger's gun, saying, 'I know we have a special cargo on-board today! You are all getting the VIP treatment.'

The children are captivated. Katie is unsure what VIP treatment means in this context. She whispers, 'Treatment' and pulls Lizzie and Benji in close to her.

A message comes over Henry's walkie-talkie. 'Safari guides in zone 3 have a sighting of a tower of giraffes at the river.'

Henry looks at the children and says, 'We'd better get moving then! Everyone into my vehicle.'

Henry drives a zebra-painted, open-top Jeep. Everyone piles in and Henry goes through the safety instructions:

'Do stay together,
Never get out of the car,
Don't feed the animals,
Don't scream,
BUT do take lots of photos!'

Kai looks at Katie and quietly says, 'This will be a big part of your African Adventure.'

Katie's mind is spinning, flashing back to the conversation about Daisy that she overheard at Granny Jojo's. What does Kai mean by this?

Addressing all the children Kai proudly says, 'Guess what, we're spending the night in this safari park!'

Katie is panic-stricken and thinks to herself, are we going to be left like Daisy was? Sami looks at Lizzie and jokes, 'You better be careful no tigers come and eat you up while you're sleeping!'

Rose pretends to swat him and says, 'Don't be silly, there are no tigers in Africa!'

Benji pipes in, 'But maybe the lions will come and get you!'

Sweetpea kindly squeezes Lizzie's hand and says, 'You know it's only baby-banter with those beastly boys.'

As the safari gets underway, Kai encourages them all to think of as many collective animal names as possible. Rose is secretly very impressed. She thinks to herself, 'Why didn't I think of that?! Such a great way to get the children learning about animal groups.'

'I don't want to blink in case I miss anything.' Lizzie is looking out of the window.

Noticing Katie isn't her usual bubbly self, Rose tries to encourage her to take photos of all the wild animals. 'Come on, Katie, why aren't you joining in? This is an amazing opportunity. This is better than anything you'll find on one of your Google image searches. I'd have thought you'd be snapping away at everything you're seeing.'

Katie's eyes are wide and Rose notices the look of anxiety on her face. Grabbing hold of Rose, Katie sobs, 'Mum, are you going to leave us here like Daisy?'

'What are you talking about, Katie?' Rose replies. 'Who's been talking to you about Daisy?' Shocked, Rose continues, 'Don't think about it now, we'll talk about it later. I promise you, I won't let anything bad happen to any of you.'

Reassured that Rose will keep them all safe, Katie joins in, coming up with the most unusual collective animal names.

A flamboyance of flamingos
A murder of crows
A congregation of alligators
A flange of baboons
A sleuth of bears
An ambush of tigers
A cackle of hyenas
A tower of giraffes
A herd of elephants
A band of gorillas

After a day of awesome animal spotting, everyone's exhausted. The Jeep drives them out of the gates and next door is their safari hotel complex. There is a self-contained bungalow with a large living room and patio doors looking out over the jungle and five bedrooms and a small kitchenette area. They all pile off to bed, but Katie creeps into Rose's room. She lies on the bed next to her and gazes into Rose's face.

Cuddling Katie, Rose whispers to her, 'I don't know what happened to Daisy, but I promise you, this is one mystery we are going to solve. We will ask Granny Jojo and Aunt Lily about it when we return.'

Katie gradually drifts off and Rose gently carries her to her own bed, which she is sharing with Lizzie. She looks over at the sleeping girls and thinks to herself, 'I'm going to make sure all you children are kept safe.'

19

Shortlisting

30 August
Sophia

Two weeks later, back at the flat in NDA's kitchen, Sophia is casually flicking through daytime TV while NDA is cooking when the phone rings.

'You won't believe this, Sophia, but we've made it to the finals of the Freedom Charity competition,' Charlie excitedly reports.

Sophia repeats his words out loud, then puts the phone on loudspeaker so NDA can hear.

'Really, you're not pulling my leg, are you? A gala dinner… with Prince Harry! Oh my God, he's so lush. Do you think we can perform our song in front of him? When can you come over and practise?' Sophia asks eagerly.

'They've given us a table of ten, so we can bring everyone!' Charlie explodes with excitement.

NDA is busy working out numbers, 'So Sophia, it's your mum, dad and Vinny. Charlie, it's your dad, your mum will come with her fella,' NDA said, trying not to sound bitter, 'and with me that makes nine,' NDA says out loud. She continues, 'We'd better invite dear Mr William Payne. After all he recorded the Freedom song and sent it off for you!'

Before Sophia and Charlie can protest, the ten places are allocated and they are both secretly looking forward to seeing the Payne again!

NDA and Sophia decide to visit the big department store in town for the best outfits of the season. Sophia takes great pleasure in telling all the lovely sales assistants, 'We're going to a dinner with Prince Harry.'

NDA has scoured Hello magazine six times and finally decided that she should wear lavender – this season's colour. In the department store, she finally settles on a pretty lavender dress with a matching jacket.

'Ohhh, you don't think it's too young for me, do you?' she frets.

'No NDA, you look proper lush. A bit like the Queen! Do you think you should get a matching hat? The Queen always wears a hat and matching gloves,' Sophia encourages NDA.

'No dear', NDA said. 'No, I think that would be a waste, especially as I can't wear a hat inside. And gloves, ohhh no, not for me! This outfit will be perfect.'

NDA looks in the mirror and sees all the sales girls cooing in agreement. She continues, 'I'd better get a matching bra and knickers while I'm out.'

'I hope they're not for Willy Payne!' Sophia thinks, laughing.

NDA ignores Sophia's giggle outburst and asks, 'Sophia dear, have you seen anything you like?'

'I'm not sure. It's going to be the biggest day of my life meeting Prince Harry. I've Googled to find out what his favourite colour is and I can't find out!' Sophia sighs. 'Besides, NDA, Mum doesn't want you to spend your money on an outfit for me.'

Sophia suddenly thinks about Mum adamantly insisting that Sophia was NOT to let NDA buy an outfit for her.

'She can't afford it on her pension,' Sophia remembered Mum and Dad explaining.

'Nonsense, my Graham has given me a few quid to treat us, so it's not my pension! Come on, let's get cracking!' NDA replies.

20

FGM Table Discussion

22 August
Katie

'I know I should be in bed; tomorrow is the day of the big party,
I know I shouldn't be looking at the camera,
I know I shouldn't be sitting on the stairs,
BUT I'm not even tired,
BUT I'm the oldest,
BUT I need to know how the pictures look for my projects,' Katie thinks to herself as she sits on a step in the middle of the staircase.

She can hear Granny Jojo with her do-do list. Even if she wanted to sleep, she'd be able to hear Granny Jojo's voice wafting up through the floorboards. Uncle Kai is bouncing, full of energy as normal. He's recounting all the safari stories to Granny Jojo and Aunt Lily. His elephant impersonations aren't just for Lizzie – Granny Jojo is now roaring with laughter. Kai is grabbing handfuls of tomorrow's party food with his make-believe trunk and secretly scooping them into his mouth. Rose is glued to the sink as usual this holiday. Kai tries to prise her away, as she playfully swots him with a tea towel.

'Kai, get the glasses out, we'll have some moonshine now the children have all gone to bed,' Granny Jojo says. She turns to Rose and says, 'Let your hair down, Rose, and have a glass. Come and tell us your tales from safari and get your wrinkly hands out of that dishwater. Did any wild animals try and grab you in the night? Or did your icy presence scare them away?'

Rose dries her hands and sits down. Lily passes her a glass of moonshine but Rose pushes it back. She says calmly but firmly, 'I need some answers.'

Turning to Lily, she says, 'Katie overheard us talking about Daisy. I need to understand how and why she died, so I can explain the truth to her.'

The light atmosphere suddenly changes. That same shiver

feeling comes over Katie again. She almost drops the camera and curls her knees to her chest. Kai turns to Rose and says, 'What's going on? What's all this about Daisy?'

'Why do you have to keep bringing up the past?' Lily says.

Granny Jojo is stunned into silence for once and stares into the distance. Without addressing anyone in particular, she says, 'Where's all this come from?' Turning to Rose, she asks, 'Why do you have to mention that beautiful girl's name?'

Lily stands up and throws her arms around her mother, glaring at Rose.

'Enough of all these secrets,' Rose says. 'I'm simply asking what happened to your twin sister!'

'Child, this happened such a long time ago. The pain still hurts me every day. It was just an unfortunate time for us all; the child just wasn't strong enough. The medicine man did all he could to save her.'

'The medicine man!' Rose spits. 'Did you not take her to a hospital? What happened to her?'

Kai suddenly leans in and asks Granny Jojo, 'I don't understand. What's going on? What happened to Daisy?'

'It was a long time ago, and it was just one of those things that happens. No one could have done anything to save her. I remember that morning as if it were yesterday. I re-live it every day. I took both the girls in to the forest. I remember the exact spot, because it's where my mother took me when I was their age. You may remember, Rose, I took you to the same spot. You remember that clearing with that little hut? Ooohhhh, my heart aches thinking about it. She was always so much smaller than the rest of you, but how could any of us have known she would get such a bad infection? It was too late; there was nothing anyone could do. I prayed and prayed for that girl to be saved.'

Looking directly at Lily, she continues, 'I swear, when I left you both you were fine. The following sunset we came to collect you both. Lily, you seemed fine, but your sister was red-hot. I remember the beads of sweat, she was dripping wet. She'd been bleeding real bad, the poor child.'

She continues, 'We all did all we could. I stayed with her night and day. The medicine man tried everything to preserve that girl's life. Child, she just died. She was weak. You know, Kai, when you have twins there is always a stronger and a weaker child and when the infection took hold there was nothing anyone could do. I never meant for any harm to come to any of my babies.'

Kai says, questioningly, 'What are you talking about, Mum?'

'If only Ivy were here, she could explain it better to you, Son. She understands all this so much better than me,' Granny Jojo replies. She continues to them all, 'It didn't make any sense because, Lily, you were fine.'

Looking at Rose, she says, 'The same as you were fine. The same as everyone is fine. No harm happened to you children. You remember the parties we had and the beautiful dresses to celebrate?' Granny Jojo babbles, trying to justify what she had put her girls through.

Katie remains on the stair with her heart in her mouth. She hears about the dresses and the party and remembers the party Ivy has planned for the weekend.

Exasperated, Rose says, 'Enough of this. Are you saying she was cut, and that's why she died?'

At that instant Katie drops her camera to the floor in shock. Everyone is startled by the noise and Rose rushes out, realising that Katie must have overheard. Rose scoops up Katie and places her on her lap in the chair at the head of the table, while Granny Jojo prepares Katie some warm goat's milk.

Rose says gently to Katie, 'I know this is difficult, but I've always told you the truth, haven't I?'

'Yes, Mum', Katie replies with tears in her eyes.

Rose cradles Katie. 'I think it's time we talked about this openly', and calmly explains to Katie what happened to her and her sisters.

'I don't remember much about what happened to me really. I vaguely remember there was a party for me and for some of the other girls. I remember I had my hair braided and I had a new dress. I remember a few of us skipping out into the forest.

'I remember hearing girls screaming. I was blindfolded and something was put in my mouth so I couldn't speak and I was held very tightly so I couldn't struggle. They cut me. I can remember how painful it was. I couldn't cry out.

'When I could speak I called for my mother to help me, but when the blindfold was removed I saw her standing over me'.

JoJo was sitting there shaking; her face had gone grey.

'Katie, Granny didn't mean to hurt me. She loves me. She loves all her children, but she was misguided and ill informed. Sometimes people who love you get it wrong.

In a daze, Katie turns to Rose and says, 'But what about the party that Aunty Ivy has organised for tomorrow? And you've got us new dresses. This is exactly the same thing that happened to Daisy. Is the same thing going to happen to…'

'I will never let anything bad like this happen to you and Lizzie,' Rose says adamantly.

'But what about Sweetpea?' Katie replies.

At that moment Ivy mysteriously appears in the kitchen doorway. Kai looks at his wife and says, 'This will NEVER happen to Sweetpea.'

Ivy stands there in disbelief; this discussion goes against the traditions and beliefs she has grown up with.

21

Gala Dinner

2 September
Sophia

NDA's mobile hairdresser has come to do their hair on the morning of the Freedom Charity gala dinner.

'Oh it's my treat, all us girls getting our hair done, it's all so proper posh.'

NDA has been fussing around and spending all Graham's money on a new outfit. The flat is suddenly filled with the sound of a horn beeping – the minibus has arrived.

BEEP BEEP, BEEEP BEEEEEEEP BEEEP BEEEP
BEEP BEEP, BEEEP BEEEEEEEP BEEEP BEEEP
BEEP BEEP, BEEEP BEEEEEEEP BEEEP BEEEP
BEEP BEEP, BEEEP BEEEEEEEP BEEEP BEEEP

NDA's son beeps the minibus' horn.

Everyone is running around excitedly. Sophia and NDA are starting to get butterflies in their stomachs at the thought of seeing their dream men. Sophia's mum Jasmine is wearing a beautiful cream sari with lavender sequins. Vinny is dressed in a cream dress with a lavender bolero and has borrowed Mum's large pearl necklace. Shekhar has a smart navy suit, blue shirt and lavender tie. Charlie bursts in, wearing a black suit and another lavender tie, which he is pulling at as if it were strangling him! His hair has been cut, but it is still as floppy as ever.

'OHHH that's lush, we match,' Sophia shrieks with delight.

'I look like a flippin' penguin,' Charlie laughs as he realises NDA has bought all the men matching lavender ties.

Sophia's dress is beautiful. Surprise, surprise, it is lavender silk with a large flowing skirt and a pretty sweetheart neckline. Her hair is beautifully curled and flows down her back. Jasmine is a little anxious about Sophia wearing any kind of high heels. Until now

Jasmine has always been very strict and only allowed the girls to wear sensible boring flat shoes. When NDA took Sophia to the department store she had given into Sophia's squeals of delight as soon as Sophia clapped eyes on the lavender sequined slip-ons. NDA wanted to treat Sophia and secretly got the assistant to wrap them. Sophia was heartbroken to leave the shoes, but NDA explained kindly, 'You know your mum would never let you wear them dear.'

But when Sophia is getting ready, NDA hands Sophia a pretty pink box.

'Go on, open it darling,' NDA was bursting with excitement.

'A present, NDA, what is it?' Sophia carefully unties the pink bow. 'OMG! You've got me the heels we saw! Oh I love them, thank you.'

Sophia jumps up and gives NDA a hug and kiss.

The commotion gradually dies down as they pile into the minibus. Charlie explains to NDA that his mum will be meeting them at the gala dinner.

'My mum and her posh fella are meeting us there, they stayed in a hotel last night,' Charlie says disappointedly. 'Mum said she wouldn't be seen dead in lavender either,' he confesses. 'And there was no way she'd be seen in a minibus,' he snorts.

'Don't worry Charlie,' NDA says, hugging her grandson. 'You've got us!' Pharell's song, Happy, is blaring out and everyone is singing merrily along.

Eventually they arrive at the hall in central London. Fremont the Freedom tiger is greeting people at the door. The security is tight and everyone is given wristbands. The flashes of phones and cameras blind them all as thousands of pictures are taken.

'I can't see him,' Sophia complains.

'Let me escort our VIPs to their table,' the smiley lady from Freedom beams.

The finalists are seated right at the front. The table has a purple tablecloth with yellow and purple balloons and there are bright gold goodie bags. The room is very grand with large windows that overlook beautifully lit gardens. Everything is gold and white. There is a huge domed ceiling with the largest chandelier any of them has ever seen. As they enter everyone takes a deep breath at such an amazing venue.

'It looks like a film set,' Sophia coos.

'It's the most beautiful room I've ever seen,' NDA says blinking and looking around.

'I'm a bit scared,' Sophia confesses to everyone.

'I know, so am I,' everyone replies in unison!

William Payne has travelled down earlier and is already sitting at the table when they arrive. He has sneakily rearranged the place settings so he can sit next to NDA!

'Oh, you look proper lovely,' he says, standing and kissing NDA on the hand. 'But I bet the food isn't half as good as your cooking,' he coos.

Everyone suddenly falls silent as they notice the commotion at the door. Even more cameras are flashing and they realise it must be the guest of honour. Prince Harry walks through the main doors, looking handsome as he smiles for the cameras. He walks through the hall and past Sophia and Charlie's table and then, as he walks onto the stage, he poses for a funny photo with Fremont. Everyone cheers.

'OMG!' Sophia squealed, 'he's matching us!'

Prince Harry is tall and handsome and much to everyone's astonishment he is wearing a navy suit and lilac tie, with his red hair flopped neatly to one side.

'I see he's wearing the tie I sent him,' NDA nudges, smiles and winks. Charlie and Sophia are both stunned!

'Really NDA, you sent Prince Harry the same tie as ours, and look, he's wearing it?' Charlie says.

'You never told me you knew him,' Sophia adds.

'Should I be a bit jealous?' Payne teases.

22

Party Prep

24 August
Katie

The following morning Katie walks bleary-eyed into the kitchen to find Rose still sitting in Granny Jojo's chair.

'Mum, have you been here all night?' Katie asks concerned.

At that moment the door swings open and a group of local women walk in, all carrying trays of party food.

Katie looks at Rose inquisitively and says, 'What's going on?'

'Oh, we're having a party for you, dear,' one neighbour says to Katie.

'Did you not know this is the day of your special party?' another adds.

Then Sweetpea bounces in wearing a vivid pink party dress. She asks, 'Why aren't you dressed yet, Katie? Everyone's almost here!'

As if by magic Ivy and Lizzie appear in the kitchen doorway. Lizzie is dressed in her brand new smart pink dress. Lizzie calls to Katie, 'Get ready, get ready! You're not dressed yet!'

Katie answers the girls, 'What's going on? I didn't think this was going to happen to anyone else! Please Mum,' Katie struggles to speak.

Lizzie and Sweetpea say in unison, 'Don't be silly Katie; it's the day of our party! Hurry up and get ready, everyone's here.'

Ivy turns to Katie and says, 'Come on Katie, I've laid your dress out upstairs.'

'ENOUGH! This is NOT happening,' Rose shouts out.

At that moment Kai bursts into the kitchen with the two boys. He's concerned after hearing his sister shout. Everyone freezes. To Katie it feels like time is standing still. Granny Jojo shoos all the children except Katie out of the kitchen and stands next to Rose at the head of the table.

Rose shouts out, 'SIT DOWN,' as she pulls Katie onto her lap.

All the local women and Kai sit down obediently. Rose addresses the full kitchen saying, 'No more girls in this village are going to be cut.'

Not all the women can accept what Rose is saying.

One of the women retorts back, 'But it's part of our religion. All women have to have this done. It keeps us clean and we remain pure – a virgin until our wedding night.'

Rose immediately challenges her.

'There is NO religion that states you have to be cut. Most women in the world are never cut. Normal basic hygiene keeps women clean. This is seen as a form of abuse elsewhere in the world. It can cause problems with intercourse when you get older.'

Some of the other women start to challenge Jojo and Rose.

Jojo's oldest friend stands to question Rose.

'Rose, girls are clean and beautiful once they've been cut. Otherwise they will turn into men.'

Rose struggles to keep a straight face as she answers, 'I am a qualified nurse in the UK and that's simply not true - it's a silly superstition. You don't believe that do you?'

The final woman says, 'But it's good for you. It makes you healthy and I know the cutting tool is washed clean.'

Rose snaps back, 'Clean is not the same as sterile! It can lead to infection and complications.'

The woman responds, 'But it's completely safe, nothing can go wrong.'

Rose sighs, 'There's a serious risk of blood loss during the cutting, of serious infection following the procedure and of longer term complications.' She pauses,

'And of death; look what happened to poor Daisy.'

'This practice is not right. There is no religion that says it needs to be done. I accept that it's part of our culture and tradition and has been going on for centuries, but we are strong women and we can stop it. All of us suffer the pain of FGM every day. Why does it take me three times longer than any uncut woman to pee?'

The women in the kitchen all nod. Kai goes up to his sister and puts his hand on her shoulder for support. Granny Jojo is at her other side. Katie thinks to herself, 'Mum has always been a boring, bossy, busybody, but today she is a modern day hero. She is reasoning, explaining and educating.'

Some women in the kitchen start to nod in agreement; they

have all suffered equally.

Granny Jojo says, 'Now most of you know, my dearest Daisy died 40 years ago today.' She holds Lily's hand tenderly with a tear in her eye. 'I'd always thought her death was unavoidable, but last night it dawned on me. If Daisy hadn't been cut, we'd have been celebrating her birthday instead of mourning her passing. No other girl should go through the pain or the ritual sacrifice of mutilation. This ends in our lifetime, this ends today.'

Looking at Kai, Ivy says, 'But this is part of our culture, men demand chastity.'

'Ridiculous! This will NOT happen in my name,' Kai states firmly.

Granny Jojo calmly but loudly repeats, 'This ends in our lifetime, this ends today!'

Rose hugs her mum and says, 'Let's have this party in Daisy's name. Let's celebrate her life. Her death has not been in vain if the barbaric practice of FGM stops today.'

The house is buzzing from the party, with various visitors coming in and out. Rose is still holding court as more and more women come to the house to discuss the issue of FGM. Mum informs them all about the possibility of surgery that could make a difference.

Granny Jojo is becoming increasingly instrumental in swaying all the sceptics and her voice fills the house. Every ten minutes you can hear her bellow, 'This stops now!'

Ivy appears in the kitchen doorway with her white scarf wafting behind her. She says, 'Come on Katie, it's your turn now.'

That same cold shiver goes down Katie's spine and she can feel her hands getting clammy. Ivy holds a rusty old red tin and the colour accentuates her long spindly witch-like fingers with glistening emerald green nail varnish tips. Katie's bottom lip is quivering uncontrollably and she thinks to herself, 'Why can't I speak?'

With a jolt she comes back to reality as Rose says, 'Katie, come on. Aunty Ivy's talking to you!'

Still shaking, Katie stutters, 'Ple-ase, p-l-ease, don't do this.'

'But Sweetpea said how much you wanted this done,' Ivy replies.

'You won't be able to get this done back at home, Katie,' Rose adds.

'But this isn't what I want,' Katie desperately pleads.

Thoughts dash through Katie's mind, 'Why has Mum betrayed me? I trusted her. The last few days have just been empty words. Who can I ask for help, if I can't trust my mum and my dad's not here? If I were at school, I could talk to a teacher. If only I had my phone on me, I could use the Freedom Charity app.'

Seeing Katie is in distress, Rose encourages her to sit in Granny Jojo's chair and says to her, 'Katie, calm down, you're acting like a baby!'

With tears in her eyes, Katie shouts out, 'Lizzie, Sweetpea! I need to make sure they're ok.'

Ivy opens the rusty old red box. Her heart beats louder and louder as Aunty Ivy reaches in and pulls something out of the tin. All Katie can see is a metal handle. Before she can see exactly what Aunty Ivy is holding, she is distracted by the commotion in the hallway.

At that moment Lizzie and Sweetpea burst in with beads bouncing brightly on their heads. Lizzie calls out with pride, 'Look, look! Look what Aunty Ivy has done to my hair. Isn't it beautiful? All the beads jangle when I move. I got all pink, but you could have multi-coloured.'

Katie looks at Aunty Ivy in relief as she says to her, 'Now Katie, what colours would you like?'

Katie looks down at the rusty red tin and sees an old metal comb and an array of brightly coloured beads and hairbands. Katie bursts into tears and turns to Rose, saying, 'I thought Aunty Ivy was going to cut me like Daisy.'

Rose wipes away Katie's tears and says, 'That will never happen to you, I promise.'

Katie hugs Rose and says, 'But it happened to you, Mum, didn't it?'

'It did, Katie, and it affected a large part of my life. When I met your father he told me about certain operations they can perform to make life easier, so fourteen years ago I had reconstructive surgery.'

Aunty Ivy looks shocked and says to Katie, 'That was the past, child. I couldn't see past tradition, but your mum and uncle have shown me that horrid, barbaric and inhumane practices of cutting our girls are carried out in the name of custom and religion. There is no need for this practice and it will never happen here again.'

The tension is shattered as Benji's bouncy ball bursts into the kitchen and sends all of Ivy's beads flying.

Granny Jojo screams, 'That ball's for boiling! Right boys, it's bead picking-up time!' Benji has caught the end of the conversation and asks, 'What girls are cut, Mum? What is Aunty Ivy talking about?' totally ignoring Granny Jojo.

'There are some practices that have been going on around here which are not right and harming girls,' Kai says. 'We are all putting a stop to this.'

They sit Benji down and explain very simply about FGM.

As the conversation draws to an end, Benji says thoughtfully,

'What can I do to help?'

'As the men in the family, we will put a stop to this through talking and education and not being afraid to talk and tell other men and boys how wrong this is,' Kai says firmly.

23

Awards

2 September
Sophia

Prince Harry takes the microphone and says, 'And the winners of the freedom song are...'

Sophia's heart is in her mouth and her palms are sweaty. The cameras flash and everything is bright white. Everyone is cheering like mad, but Sophia's nerves had stopped her from hearing the all-important outcome!

'Go on,' Dad says encouragingly.

'What?' Sophia replies.

'You've won!'

Dad cheers. Everyone roars.

Prince Harry shakes Charlie's hand and says, 'Well done, mate, great song!'

Sophia is standing to the side and as Prince Harry bends down to shake her hand she throws her arms around him and gives him a gigantic hug. She beams the broadest smile on earth and Prince Harry smiles back. The three of them are standing hand in hand on the stage, looking out proudly. Fremont has lost all decorum and is dancing around them madly.

Sophia is shaking but she successfully makes it back to her seat. She and Charlie are both holding matching iPads and a certificate signed by Prince Harry himself!

Shekhar is overwhelmed; he's lost for words and has to fight back the tears. He just manages to mouth, 'Love you, my princess!'

'I'm so proud, I could burst,' Mum says.

'Well done, Sis,' Vinny says proudly.

'That's my boy,' Charlie's dad exclaims.

'He takes after me,' his mum gloats.

'The kids all done good,' NDA says quietly to Willy Payne.

As they sit down William Payne hands them both purple covers for their new iPads. It was as if he knew they were going to win!

As pudding comes round, Charlie and Sophia sing out in unison, 'Oh, I am partial to pudding!'

The laughter and celebrations continue right into the small hours.

24

The Hut

26 August
Katie

Rose screams up the stairs, 'Lizzie, Benji, come on. Everyone is waiting for you!'

Turning to Kai, she says, 'Quick! Have you got their suitcases down yet?'

Kai says, 'Chill out! You've got at least 12 hours before your flight leaves!' He turns to Katie and picks her up, throwing her onto his shoulders in one move. Kai then turns back to Rose, picks her up in his arms and spins her around. At that instant a herd of elephants trundles down the stairs. The twins run out and scream, 'Pile on,' and all the children jump on Uncle Kai.

Granny Jojo comes over, unpicks the children one by one and says to them all with a glint in her eye, 'You're going to have one decent meal before you go. God knows how long it'll be before your next one, plus we all know how good your mum's cooking is.'

She pulls out the twins first as they are still squealing and wriggling with delight. She gives them each a big sloppy kiss and sits them down on the bench in the kitchen. She says to them, 'You two are the lucky ones. Good cooking, day-in, day-out.'

She then turns directly to Lizzie and says, 'My, my little girl, we've grown ya like the runner beans in this African sun! And I didn't even have to put you in a pot and water ya!'

She sits Lizzie at the bench and gives her a bowlful of food, then unpicks Benji from climbing-frame Kai. He hugs her tightly round the neck and says, 'Granny Jojo, can't I just stay and live with you?'

She pulls out a chair opposite Lizzie for Benji to sit at and gives him a mountain of food to munch his way through.

She tenderly pulls Katie off Uncle Kai's shoulders and hugs her tightly. Katie says, 'But when will we see you again, Granny Jojo?'

'I might not have my own wings to fly, but there's a big-bird aeroplane I'll be getting on this time next summer! Now sit down with your brother and sister and enjoy some proper cooking.'

Aunty Ivy fills a tray with tall glasses filled with mango nectar and ice cubes and gives her a gigantic hug.

Granny Jojo turns to Rose and says, 'I'll come to the airport and see you off.' Rose beams with happiness and everyone cheers. Kai lifts his mother high into the air and says, 'You're amazing, Mumma!'

With his free arm he gives Rose a high-five and says, 'You've shaken a lot of things up around here, Sis, but in a good way!'

Aunty Lily turns to Rose and says, 'No cobwebs, no secrets. I don't think Mum's left the village in the last five years!'

'My Rose has taught me that there are a lot of things that need to change around here!' Granny Jojo proudly exclaims.

Kai carries his mother to her chair at the head of the table and she symbolically returns to her role as the head of the household.

Aunty Ivy thinks to herself, 'My, how things have changed!' She says to Rose, 'Thank goodness you've managed to restore some mealtime order in this household.'

Granny Jojo nods and says to Kai, 'Yes, sit up straight boy.'

When everyone has finished, the children collect the plates and put them in the sink.

Katie turns to Rose and says, 'Now, who would've imagined that happening two weeks ago?!'

After lunch the bag-packing mayhem continues and Katie goes to Granny Jojo and says, 'May I go and cut some flowers from the yard, please?'

Granny Jojo looks at her inquisitively and nods. She passes Katie the secateurs and signals to Aunt Lily to go and help her. Lily and Katie head out to the yard and cut an array of beautiful bright blooms for a brilliant bouquet.

With nine hours to spare, Rose rushes everyone into the minibus. Granny Jojo demands the front seat next to Uncle Kai and squeezes in between him and Rose. As they drive through the gates Kai hops out to padlock the compound shut; it is the first time in five years that the house has been completely empty!

Benji calls out from the backseat, 'Can you put some beats on Uncle Kai?'

Granny Jojo leans in and puts an old classic on.

Here's a little song I wrote
You might want to sing it note for note
Don't worry, be happy
In every life we have some trouble
When you worry you make it double
Don't worry, be happy
Don't worry, be happy now
Oo, oo-oo-oo, oo-oo-oo, oo-oo-oo-oo-oo-oo
Don't worry Oo-oo-oo-oo-oo-oo-oo
Be happy Oo-oo-oo-oo-oo o-oo-oo-oo-oo-oo-oo-oo py

Uncle Kai agrees to take a detour after a request from Katie and just outside the village he drives down a dusty track next to the forest. Everyone is so involved in singing and dancing in their seats that no one notices. The track is so dusty it blows up a big cloud of smoke around the vehicle, making it difficult for anyone to see out. They pull up in a clearing and all pile out. It smells like there is a bonfire and soon they all notice the smouldering mound.

Granny Jojo bursts out, 'What's happened to the hut? Who's responsible?'

Kai and Ivy stand together and say, 'Mumma, we are.'

Ivy adds, 'We burned it so that it can never be used for that evil act again.'

Katie turns to Aunty Lily and hands her the bouquet of flowers, which Lily puts down on the ground with a tear in her eye – finally laying to rest the ghost of her dead twin. She looks at Katie and says, 'These are the last cut flowers that are going to be left here.'

The family all pile back into the minibus and leave behind the cremated remains, content in the knowledge that the practice of FGM will never be performed in their village again.

As they approach passport control, Granny Jojo is overcome with emotion and is in floods of tears. All the children are crying as well. Even Benji has a tear in his eye about the thought of leaving Granny Jojo and his newfound family.

Granny Jojo hugs her daughter and says to her, 'You have three beautiful children. I am so proud of you and everything you have achieved.'

Rose answers with a tear in her eye, 'I learned from the best, Mumma.'

Granny Jojo gives all the children a big hug and says, 'I promise to come and visit you next summer.'

She says to Katie, 'I need you to look after my beautiful family for me.'

Katie beams with pride, and answers, 'Of course I will, Granny!'

With an hour to spare the four of them rush through customs

Having cleared UK customs, the tired travellers walk in a daze towards the airport exit. Benji rushes ahead and opens the double doors. Lizzie breaks free from Rose's hand and sees a massive Fremont tiger toy being waved at her. She squeals in excitement as Dad's arms wrap round and lift her up. She finds herself squashed between fluffy Fremont and Dad. Katie and Benji run up shortly after and pile on the pair of them, catching Dad off balance.

'Ooooohhhhh, watch it! Haven't you guys grown? Granny Jojo's cooking must be as good as Mum says; you've all got so much bigger!'

Rose turns up two minutes later with all the baggage and Dad rushes over and embraces her tenderly. Dad turns to Benji and says, 'You've done such a good job of looking after all the girls.'

Looking at Katie and Benji, he says, 'I've got special treats for you as well.'

He hands them both small black boxes. The two open them excitedly in unison and both shriek with delight, 'iWatch!!!!'

Mum looks at him in despair and mouths, 'iWatches?! How much?'

Dad, an expert in diffusing situations quickly, opens the present he has bought for Rose and speedily places the beautiful necklace round her neck. As he is fastening the clasp, he whispers in her ear, 'I've missed you.'

The three children and Fremont squash into the back of the car and before the car pulls out of the airport car park they are sound asleep.

Rose turns to Steve and says, 'Oh my, the three of them are so exhausted they are fast asleep. None of them could sleep on the plane, because they were so excited to see you. You know, you really shouldn't have spoilt them like that. I hate to think how much it all cost and the house surely isn't big enough for a life-sized Fremont?'

Katie is only dozing in the back and half-hears the conversation between Mum and Dad. She thinks to herself, 'So a necklace isn't spoiling then, is it, Mum?!'

Rose and Steve chat away about the African adventure and Steve asks, 'Do you really think there was any risk of Jojo cutting our Lizzie and Katie?'

Katie overhears and feels that familiar shiver run down her spine. Her heart is racing and she grabs hold of the door handle. She holds it so tightly her knuckles turn white.

Rose replies, 'I'm not 100% sure if Jojo wanted to perform FGM on our girls, but I'm convinced Ivy had arranged for Sweetpea's cutting and that's why she'd organised the big party. Ivy is so into tradition and superstition. Actually, for Jojo and Ivy it would have been the perfect opportunity to perform FGM on all three girls at the same time. As they'd paid for the cutter to do Sweetpea, it would have made sense for them to get three for the price of one. You know what money is like out there. It was a miracle we were visiting when we did. If we hadn't gone at that time, we wouldn't have been able to prevent it happening to little Sweetpea. And do you know, poor Kai had no idea any of this was going on!'

Steve continues, 'Do you reckon the burning of the hut is just symbolic? Or do you think it truly is the end of FGM in the village?'

Rose replies, 'I truly believe it's over; so many women in the village approached me about the possibility of reconstructive surgery. These are conversations they were afraid of having before we turned up. The thing is, unless we find alternative work for the cutters they are just going to continue this barbaric practice secretly. The whole thing will just be driven underground. FGM has been against the law for many years, but so far there have been very few prosecutions. Something needs to change.'

Steve nods his head in agreement and says, 'Men have a really important role in stopping this. We need to change their perceptions. If we can convince men that an uncut wife is more desirable, FGM will end.'

As they pull up at the house, Steve gently takes Rose's hand and says, 'I'm so proud of you, darling, and I have so missed you.'

From that moment on, Katie knows that the Smith family will be embarking on a lifelong crusade against the barbaric practice of FGM.

25

Back home

4 September 2016
Katie and Sophia

'But Vinny, it's not fair, can't you tidy up the room before Katie comes?' Sophia's side of the room is immaculate with all her scrunchies and gel pens laid out in order. On Vinny's side of the room there is a pile of dirty washing and schoolbooks.

'Oh my god, you've turned the room into a pigsty! I hate having to share a room with my pig of a sister!' Vinny calmly responds and points to a sign under her interactive Freedom poster which states, Keep calm and don't tidy up. It's known as the housework versus homework battle at home.

'Oh, can't you put my hair in a French plait?' Sophia asks Vinny.

Vinny agrees, knowing it will distract Sophia from the big tidy. She starts plaiting Sophia's long hair and leans over her desk to reach for the scrunchies, which are crammed in the same box as all the Freedom triangle badges.

Sophia starts fussing around with the handheld mirror and inspects Vinny's handiwork. She says, 'Vinny, this really isn't good enough, there are bits sticking up everywhere!'

Vinny responds, 'You're even becoming OCD about strands of hair! It's not like we've got royalty coming to visit! Katie isn't going to care about what your hair looks like, she's just here to visit you!'

'I just wanted everything to look perfect for when Katie gets here. You know she's got her own room – complete with that black chandelier I showed you,' Sophia whines.

Sophia's bottom lip starts to quiver and Vinny calmly says, 'Don't be a baby about it. We'll get it all sorted before Katie arrives.'

Sophia snaps back, 'I'm not touching your disgusting, disease-ridden, dirty drawers,' as she kicks them into a pile. She continues, 'I'll start with the desk.' She leans over to the pile of scrunchies and badges and starts sorting them. She organises the Freedom charity badges, so they are all lined up along the desk. The scrunchies are piled high in an embroidered box that used to belong to Mum. Meanwhile, Vinny's busy loading the washing machine with all her dirty clothes.

She calls out to Sophia, 'I'm just too busy to be worrying about all this trivial tidying! Life's just too short to be faffing around with this!'

Sophia cunningly says to Vinny, 'I'll do you a deal, you complete my summer holiday project and I'll do your share of the housework for the next 24 hours.'

Vinny replies, 'Make it the next week and you might have a deal!'

With the agreement sorted, Sophia meticulously tidies up the bedroom. The room is a mad frenzy as she dances around with Henry Hoover, who she has recently nicknamed Prince Henry Hoover. As Sophia is adding the finishing touches to the room, the doorbell rings. Sophia sprints to the door and proudly beams at Katie.

Mum and Dad are in the kitchen and Dad asks, 'Can I make you girls a strawberry and banana milkshake?'

Sophia answers, 'I think Katie would prefer a coke-float.'

Dad replies, 'Is it not you who wants a coke-float, Sophia?!'

With coke-floats in hand, both girls head into Vinny and Sophia's bedroom. Vinny is sat at the recently polished desk working on her coursework. Katie instantly notices the photo of Sophia with Prince Harry!

Sophia spends the next forty minutes gushing and exaggerating about the gala dinner with Prince Harry. She is convinced he is in love with her and has already planned the wedding and is now going on about what colour hair their children would have! Black + red = ?

Up until now, the perfectly patient Vinny has been tutting quietly to herself, but then she finally snaps, 'Sophia, you can't honestly believe he's interested in you!'

Vinny turns to Katie and asks, 'So how is your summer project going?'

'It's going quite well' Katie answers modestly. 'But I'm trying to make it interactive so it's taking longer than I hoped,' Katie said honestly.

Sophia sighs, 'The highlight of my holiday was spending a few hours with Prince Harry, but the rest was so-oo boring compared to

Katie's. She's had the most amazing time. She went on safari and saw all the wild animals – a proper African adventure.'

Vinny says, 'Why don't you get up the images on both your iPads? We can then compare Katie's vacation with your staycation, Sophia!'

Katie has over 500 images and short film clips of beautiful African landscapes and animals already loaded into a magnificent slideshow. Sophia looks at the images and mimics the presentation she imagines Katie giving at school, 'Dear Mrs Metcalfe, I'd like to introduce Katie Smith's Great African Adventure. Katie, her sister, brother and mum went on the trip of a lifetime to meet her Granny Jojo in Africa. Africa has 54 countries and a population of over a billion.' Sophia reels off the facts from Katie's slideshow presentation.

Sophia clicks on the next few slides. There are various amazing landscapes and an image of a beautiful desert with peaks as far as the eye can see. The last slide is a film clip of a pile of ash and smouldering rubble. As that image appears, Katie starts quivering and bursts into tears. Vinny leans over to comfort her. It's obvious something is seriously wrong. Sophia looks mortified and says, 'I'm sorry, was it something I said?'

In between sobs, Katie struggles to get the words out, as this is the first time she has been able to talk about the trauma and fear she experienced while she was staying with Granny Jojo. Looking at the remains of the burnt hut, Sophia says, 'Did someone die there?'

Katie looks up and says to Sophia, 'My aunt died in that hut. This is where they took young girls, babies practically, and women came in and cut them.'

Sophia mouths, 'Cut them? What do you mean – they were stabbed?'

'No, her flower was cut,' Katie continues.

As Vinny hands Katie some tissues she says, 'They took her womanhood away?'

'Yes. Oh Vinny, it was awful. I thought they were going to do it to my sister and me. My aunt was definitely going to perform it on my cousin. They had planned everything, even the after-party.'

Vinny pulls Katie close to her and says, 'Did they hurt you?'

Sophia says, 'Honestly Katie, you can trust Vinny.'

'When Lily and Daisy were two they were taken to the hut and blindfolded. Another woman came and held them down and they were each cut. They cried out in agony for their mother to return and help them. They couldn't believe she would just leave them there. To their disgust, when the blindfolds were removed, their mother was standing there watching the abhorrent procedure. Their legs were bound and the cutter used thorns to stitch up the wound,' Katie reveals.

Sophia puts her hands over her mouth, feeling like she is going to be sick. Vinny holds Katie's hand, encouraging her to continue.

'Lily lived, but Daisy died,' Katie continues. 'That happened over forty years ago and since then they have been doing it to every girl in the village. Had my mum not been there, they would have done it to my sister and me.'

'Oh my god, that's terrifying,' Vinny says holding Katie's hands tighter.

Sophia was shaking a little and crying softly. 'But you're OK? They haven't done anything to hurt you, have they?'

'No, we're fine. The image of the burning hut symbolises that FGM will never be practised again in our village.'

Katie continues, 'I'm so scared for the other girls who are taken on holiday to have this barbaric practice done to them. Not all of them will have a mother to protect them like me. Vinny, what can we do to stop this?'

Chapter 26

Last Note

21 September 2016
Katie and Sophia

'I can't believe your project is being turned into a school assembly,' Sophia says excitedly.

'I can't believe Tony Lee asked such an interesting question!', Katie said smiling at Sophia. 'I'm pleased that boys think it's an issue that affects them too and that they feel they can be part of the campaign to stop FGM.'

'How could I protect my sister if my mum and dad were going to cut her?' Tony Lee had asked sincerely.

'Thankfully Vinny answered that one', Sophia said proudly.

'Yes - tell a teacher or contact Freedom Charity', they chorused together.

Katie blushes. 'I didn't know the school would take it so seriously.'

The reporter looks down at her notebook and writes, 'Katie's story is so moving that a school assembly was organised to show how a young girl really can change history.'

At the end of the assembly there is a big photograph of all the students holding up copies of But It's Not Fair and Cut Flowers. That evening there is a double-page spread in the National paper By Ros about Katie's story.

That evening the Smith family plus Charlie and William Payne are invited round to Vinny and Sophia's home for a celebratory meal and screening of the news broadcast. Rose presents Jasmine with a bouquet of cut flowers, consisting of daisies, lilies, roses and sweetpeas, all tied with ivy.

William Payne arrives and hands over two bottles of fizz to Shekhar and a life-sized canvas showing Sophia hugging Prince Harry. NDA has made enough cakes for a bake sale and every visible surface is filled with scrumptious, splendid sweet treats. As Payne spies them and winks at NDA, Sophia and Charlie shout out in unison, 'OOOOHHH I'M PARTIAL TO A FAIRY CAKE!'

Everyone gathers around the TV waiting excitedly. As Chazza appears on the screen, NDA gushes from her armchair, 'Ooooooh Chazza!'

Chazza starts, 'Today, at a secondary school in east London, we have witnessed how young adults are striving to end FGM in this lifetime. We have two interviews with students: Vinny, a Freedom Charity ambassador; and Katie Smith, a girl who has already stopped FGM in her family's village.'

The cameras pan to Vinny, and Chazza asks about her role in today's events.

Vinny answers, 'As a young ambassador for Freedom Charity, I have worked with my school to host an awareness day to stop FGM. By wearing the red triangle, you too can be part of our campaign against FGM.'

The camera then turns to Katie and there is a split-screen image of the burnt hut.

Katie explains, 'On a visit to Africa this summer, this hut was burnt down. Its burning symbolises the end of FGM in my family's village. I know that through education we can stop FGM in our lifetime.'

The clip continues to show video taken in the school assembly. As the camera pans out, Sophia is seen smiling broadly as the Freedom song fades out in the background.

Everyone shouts out, 'Well done, you amazing girls!'

Katie's dad picks her up triumphantly and gives her a big proud hug.

Sophia cries out excitedly, 'Did you see me?'

Vinny, Mum and Dad all look at each other and Dad says,

'Yes, you're a star too, my dear!'

'It's just not fair,' says Sophia.

'Sophia, what now?' demand Mum and Dad together.

'It's not fair, I wish everyone could have friends and family like me'

'Awe Sofia' everyone smiles.

The End

Phew, well done you have made it to the end of the book!

I am guessing not all of you are like me and take a peek at the ending first?

I hope Cut Flowers inspires you to do something to help stop FGM and other human right abuses.

I know some of you are using this book in school and your amazing teachers will be working on some lessons around FGM with you.

The following pages of the book are for professionals.

I have asked 'the professionals' to add some help pages in for teachers, doctors, social workers, nurses and anyone working on the front line. They are designed as a guide to FGM and a reference point.

Help pages on FGM

Detective Constable 9773 Gillian Squires
Subject Matter Expert – Female Genital Mutilation (SME)
Birmingham Multi Agency Safeguarding Hub (MASH)

To readers:

I have talked to many women (and men) about FGM. I remember attending my first community event as a professional, and overtly having FGM leaflets on display. I expected it to be very quiet, and to not be approached by anyone. I was very wrong! I was delighted that I had very many deep conversations about FGM, and was approached by the vast majority of attendees, who were very open and willing to share their own experiences and had a desire to help stop this practice. Please do not be afraid of speaking about this. Make yourself familiar with terms used by different countries for FGM, so that you can use them to be understood, but also to assist in building the trust and confidence of individuals, as you show that you have an interest in the matter, and have been concerned enough to find out the relevant terminology. Individuals are very often happy to talk about the issue, so don't be afraid to speak.

There are many ways in which a girl/woman can be protected from having FGM. The Police, Children's Social Care, Non-Government Organisations can all help children and women to be safe, and to keep any other girls they are concerned about safe. The procedure to obtain a Female Genital Mutilation Protection Order (FGMPO) is simple, it is free to apply, and in fact the individual themselves can apply for the order if they so wish. The order can also be used where children are believed to have been taken abroad and are at risk of FGM. The FGMPO can order that the children are repatriated to the UK. This has already been achieved successfully, with the children not having been cut, and now being protected from future harm by the order.

To professionals:

If you have information about a cutter who is operating here in the UK, despite how little information you have about their identity, or exact whereabouts; let the Police know! Your information may be the last piece in the jigsaw. Prevention is so much better than prosecution – help the police to prevent this happening by helping to prosecute the cutters. Communities may hold valuable information and someone may be willing to inform you if and where this is happening in the UK. If they don't want to tell you, they won't, but if you don't ask, we will never know.

FGM is child abuse. However it can be different to some other forms of child abuse, as it is not seen by perpetrators as an act of hate. Families may well be otherwise caring, loving families and there may be no other warning indicators giving concern to professionals. If you are concerned about a child being at risk of FGM, or having undergone FGM, it is your responsibility to act. Child protection is everyone's responsibility. There is no place for cultural sensitivity, I hear so often about professionals having concerns about making a referral because they are worried about allegations of being racist. Document everything, you can never be criticised if you have the best interests of the child at the centre of your decision-making.

Dr Comfort Momoh MBE
FGM and public health specialist at Guy's and St Thomas' NHS Foundation Trust.

WHAT IS FEMALE GENITAL MUTILATION (FGM)?

FGM is the partial or total removal of external female genitalia for non-medical reasons. It's also known as female circumcision, cutting or sunna.

WHERE DOES FGM HAPPEN?

FGM is prevalent in Africa, the Middle East and Asia. In the UK, FGM tends to occur in areas with larger populations of communities who practise FGM, such as first-generation immigrants, refugees and asylum seekers. These areas include London, Cardiff, Manchester, Sheffield, Northampton, Birmingham, Oxford, Crawley, Reading, Slough and Milton Keynes.

WHY IS IT DONE?

Communities that practise FGM put forward many reasons and beliefs for the practice. Some of the most common misconceptions about FGM are that it promotes chastity, prevents promiscuity and helps to secure a good marriage for one's daughter. Other beliefs are that FGM is often considered a necessary part of raising a girl properly, and as a way to prepare her for adulthood and marriage, that it is beneficial for the girl or woman and that it will reduce a woman's libido and discourage sexual activity before marriage.

FGM has no medical or health benefit.

FGM procedures are irreversible and their effects last a lifetime. FGM is illegal in the UK. It is also illegal to arrange for a child to be taken abroad for FGM. If caught, offenders face a large fine and a prison sentence of up to 14 years.

ARE THERE ANY PHYSICAL/ BEHAVIOURAL WARNING SIGNS?

Warning signs of FGM include, having difficulty walking, sitting or standing and spending longer than normal using the toilet. Some individuals may behave unusually after an absence from school or college, or may be reluctant to go through normal examinations or might not want to take part in PE or swimming due to embarrassment, fear or other emotional trauma.

WHAT ARE THE SIGNS THAT A CHILD MAY BE AT RISK OF FGM?

There are signs that can guide professionals in identifying a child who might be at risk of FGM: Does the family belong to an FGM community? Are they planning a vacation or absence from school or has the girl's mother had FGM? Sometimes the child might tell her friends or a teacher at school about a 'special procedure or ceremony' that is going to take place. Girls are at particular risk of FGM during summer holidays.

WHAT TO DO IF YOU HAVE UNDERGONE FGM?

If you have undergone FGM and need help and support, you can contact clinics and support by either searching online for FGM clinics or requesting support or information from your GP. It is important to seek help when you need help. There is no need to feel embarrassed to ask.

The NSPCC supports women and girls who have undergone FGM. There are also around16 clinics now in the UK that provide support, counselling, advice and deinfibulation (also known as reversals of Type 3 FGM).

There are also survivors groups and non-governmental organisations that provides support to women and their families which you can also find online using google. If you are not a professional but are concerned for your own welfare please consider looking up these help pages somewhere private where the pages/search terms cannot be traced by the likely perpetrator.

If you are also worried about someone who is at risk of FGM or has had FGM, you must share this information with social services or the police. It is then their responsibility to investigate and protect anyone affected or likely to be affected.

ADVICE

The following pages contain information for anyone who may come across FGM, in both their personal and/or professional capacities. Some information is aimed specifically at health and social care professionals and teachers. Broadly, the information covers:

- What FGM is;
- Possible symptoms of FGM;
- How to s eek help if you or someone you know is affected by FGM; and
- The legal position on FGM.

FGM, sometimes known as 'female circumcision' or 'female genital cutting', is illegal in the UK.

It's also illegal to take abroad a British national or permanent resident for FGM, or to help someone trying to do this.

You can get up to 14 years in prison for carrying out FGM or helping it to take place.

IF THERE'S IMMEDIATE DANGER

Contact the police if you or someone you know is in immediate danger of FGM.

You should also contact the Foreign and Commonwealth Office if you know a British national who's already been taken abroad.

Foreign and Commonwealth Office

Telephone: **020 7008 1500**
From overseas: **+44 (0)20 7008 1500**
Find out about call charges

If you're abroad you can contact the nearest British embassy, commission or consulate.

IF YOU OR SOMEONE YOU KNOW IS AT RISK

Contact the NSPCC anonymously if you're worried that a girl or young woman is at risk or is a victim of FGM.

NSPCC FGM Helpline

Email: **fgmhelp@nspcc.org.uk**
Telephone: **0800 028 3550**
From overseas: **+44 (0)800 028 3550**
Find out about call charges

TYPES OF FGM

FGM comprises all procedures involving partial or total removal of the external female genitalia or other injury to the female genital organs for non-medical reasons. Broadly, FGM has been categorised by the World Health Organisation into four widely recognised types (although not all cases of FGM fall within these types):

Type 1: Partial or total removal of the clitoris and/or the prepuce (clitoridectomy)

Type 2: Partial or total removal of the clitoris and the labia minora, with or without excision of the labia majora (excision)

Type 3: Narrowing of the vaginal opening through the creation of a covering seal. The seal is formed by cutting and repositioning the inner or outer labia with or without removal of the clitoris (infibulation)

Type 4: All other harmful procedures to the female genitalia for non-medical purposes, for example: pricking, piercing, incising, scraping and cauterising the genital area.

FGM AWARENESS

FGM may not be referred to explicitly – listen out for discussions around:

- Going on an extended holiday to a country which practices the procedure[1]
- Going to have a 'special procedure' or 'celebration'
- Going to 'become a woman'

Other indications that FGM may be about to take place:

[1] In descending order of prevalence, the main countries in which FGM is practised are: Somalia, Guinea, Djibouti, Egypt, Eritrea, Mali, Sierra Leone, Sudan, Gambia, Burkina Faso, Ethiopia, Mauritania, Liberia, Guinea-Bissau, Chad, Côte d'Ivoire, Kenya, Nigeria, Senegal, Central African Republic, Yemen, United Republic of Tanzania, Benin, Iraq, Ghana, Togo, Niger, Cameroon, Uganda. Note that this is not an exhaustive list

- If a female elder is present in the family home, visiting from a practising country[2]
- Going on an extended holiday to a practicing country
- A girl may confide that she is going to have a 'special procedure' 'operation' or small injection
- Correcting perceived 'westernised/bad behaviour', continuing education in country of origin
- Parents seeking to withdraw their child(ren) from learning about FGM.

One of the most common ways to get a child abroad is to tell the child a relative is sick and/or dying. Sickness, death and funerals are a very common excuse/reason for travel.

POSSIBLE SIGNS/SYMPTOMS THAT A GIRL/WOMAN HAS ALREADY HAD FGM

- A girl/woman has difficulty walking, sitting or standing and may appear to be uncomfortable.
- A girl/woman spends longer than normal in the toilet due to difficulties. menstruating/urinating. They may suffer UTI's and they will be reoccurring
- A girl/woman has frequent urinary, menstrual or stomach problems.
- There may be frequent absences from school or college.

- Withdrawal or depression or significant behavioural change.
- Reluctance to undergo medical examinations.
- A girl may talk about pain or discomfort between her legs.
- Not partaking in physical exercise.
- Long absences from school, being removed early prior to a holiday or returned late.
- Conforming to traditional dress.

POSSIBLE SHORT TERM SYMPTOMS

Immediate effects of FGM can include:
- severe pain and bleeding;
- emotional and psychological shock;
- haemorrhage;

[2]See FN1 above.

- wound infections, including tetanus and blood-borne viruses (including HIV and Hepatitis B and C);
- urinary retention;
- injury to adjacent tissues;
- fracture or dislocation as a result of restraint;
- damage to other organs; and
- in some cases, death.

Almost all females who undergo FGM experience pain and bleeding as a consequence of the procedure. The event is of itself traumatic, as girls are held down during the procedure. Risk and complications increase with the type of FGM and are more severe and prevalent with infibulations.

POSSIBLE LONG TERM SYMPTOMS

The long term consequences of FGM can include:

- chronic vaginal and pelvic infections;
- difficulties with menstruation;
- difficulties in passing urine and chronic urine infections;
- renal impairment and possible renal failure;
- damage to the reproductive system, including infertility;
- infibulation cysts, neuromas and keloid scar formation;
- obstetric fistula;
- complications in pregnancy and delay in the second stage of childbirth;
- pain during sex and lack of pleasurable sensation;
- psychological damage, including a number of mental health and psychosexual problems such as low libido, depression, anxiety and sexual dysfunction; flashbacks; substance misuse and self-harm;
- reduced attendance at cervical screening appointments, and delaying seeking treatment for other conditions as a result of wishing to hide FGM;
- increased risk of HIV and other sexually transmitted infections; and/or
- death of mother and child during childbirth

Where a FGM survivor gives birth, the scar tissue might tear, or the opening may need to be cut to allow the baby to come out. After childbirth, women from some prevalent communities may be sewn up again to make them "tight" for their husband (reinfibulation). Such cutting and re-stitching of a woman's genitalia results in painful scar tissue.

FGM IS ILLEGAL

FGM is illegal in England and Wales under the Female Genital Mutilation Act 2003[3]. Parts of this Act also apply in Northern Ireland. In Scotland, FGM legislation is contained in the Prohibition of Female Genital Mutilation (Scotland) Act 2005. Under the Female Genital Mutilation Act 2003 (the 2003 Act), a person is guilty of an offence if they excise, infibulate or otherwise mutilate the whole or any part of a girl's labia majora, labia minora or clitoris. The 2003 Act also provides that the term "girl" includes "woman" so the offences in sections 1 to 3 apply to victims of any age.

Other than in excepted circumstances set out in the 2003 Act, it is an offence for any person (regardless of their nationality or residence status) to:

- perform FGM in England or Wales;
- assist a girl to carry out FGM on herself in England or Wales; or
- assist (from England or Wales) a non-UK national or UK resident to carry out FGM outside the UK on a UK national or UK resident[4].

Provided therefore that the FGM takes place in England or Wales, the nationality or residence status of the victim is irrelevant.

A person may also be guilty of an offence under the 2003 Act if they have failed to protect a girl from the risk of FGM. This means that if an offence under sections 1, 2 or 3 of the 2003 Act has been committed against a girl under the age of 16, each person who is responsible for the girl at the time the FGM occurred could be liable under the offence. Those who have parental responsibility and the means by which they can acquire it are set out in the Children Act 1989 (in the case of England and Wales). This includes, for example:

- a child's biological mother;
- a father who is married to the mother of the child when the child is born;
- an unmarried father registered on the child's birth certificate at the time of their birth;
- guardians; and
- persons named in a Child Arrangements Order.
- In addition, the 2003 Act also makes it an offence for a UK national or UK resident to:
- perform FGM outside the UK;
- assist a girl to perform FGM on herself outside the UK; and

---

[3]As amended by sections 70-75, Serious Crime Act 2015
[4]a "UK resident" is defined as an individual who is habitually resident in the UK

- assist (from outside the UK) a non-UK national or UK resident to carry out FGM outside the UK on a UK national or UK resident.

An offence of failing to protect a girl from the risk of FGM may also be committed wholly or partly outside the UK by a UK national or UK resident.

Under provisions of the law which apply generally to criminal offences, it is also an offence to

- aid, abet, counsel or procure a person to commit an FGM offence;
- encourage or assist a person to commit an FGM offence;
- attempt to commit an FGM offence; and
- conspire to commit an FGM offence.

The 2003 Act also places a mandatory duty on health and social care professionals and teachers in England and Wales to report known cases of FGM in under 18s which they identify in the course of their professional work to the police (mandatory reporting).

In addition, the 2003 Act provides for the making of FGM Protection Orders in England and Wales. An FGM Protection Order is a civil law measure which may be made for the purposes of protecting a girl at risk of FGM or protecting a girl against whom an FGM offence has been committed. Breach of an FGM Protection Order is a criminal offence (FGM Protection Orders).

MANDATORY REPORTING – GUIDANCE FOR PROFESSIONALS

The FGM mandatory reporting duty is a legal duty provided for in the FGM Act 2003 (as amended by the Serious Crime Act 2015). The legislation requires regulated health and social care professionals and teachers in England and Wales to report known cases of FGM in under 18s to the police.

The purpose of the duty is to help make sure that professionals have the confidence to confront FGM and to help increase the number of referrals to the police so that cases can be investigated appropriately.

Procedural information for professionals is available on GOV.
UK: **www.gov.uk/government/uploads/system/uploads/
attachment_data/file/469448/FGM-Mandatory-Reporting-
procedural-info-FINAL.pdf**

ARE YOU REQUIRED TO MAKE A REPORT?

From 31 October 2015, certain professionals in England and Wales
have a mandatory reporting duty in relation to FGM.

The duty applies to you if you are a regulated health or social care
professional or teacher in England and Wales.

Non-regulated practitioners also have a responsibility to take
appropriate safeguarding action in relation to any identified or
suspected case of FGM, in line with wider safeguarding frameworks.

WHAT DO YOU NEED TO DO?

You must make a report to the police if:
- a girl under 18 has told you that they have had FGM; or
- you observe physical signs which appear to show that an act
  of FGM has been carried out on a girl under 18 and they have
  no reason to believe that the act was necessary for the girl's
  physical or mental health or for purposes connected with labour
  or birth.

Your duty to report applies if the individual is under 18 years old at
the time of the disclosure/identification of FGM. If the individual is
over 18 years old, follow local safeguarding procedures.

The duty does not apply in relation to at risk or suspected cases.
Always ask your local safeguarding lead if in doubt.

Remember that, in addition to complying with the duty, professionals
should continue to have regard to their wider safeguarding
responsibilities, which require consideration and action to be taken
whenever there is any identified or known risk to a child or vulnerable
adult, whether in relation to FGM or another matter.

WHEN AND HOW MUST YOU MAKE A REPORT?

- Call 101 as soon as possible; normally by close of the next working day.
- Longer timeframes are allowed under exceptional circumstances but always discuss with your local safeguarding lead.

WHY MUST YOU MAKE A REPORT?

- The duty is a personal duty which requires the individual professional who becomes aware of the case to make a report; the responsibility cannot be transferred.
- For health and social care professionals, failure to comply with the duty may be considered through fitness to practise proceedings by the regulator with whom the professional is registered.
- For teachers, schools will need to consider any failure to comply with the duty in accordance with their staff disciplinary procedures.

REMEMBER:

- Record all decisions/actions
- Be prepared for a police officer to call you back
- Update your local safeguarding lead
- You will have to provide:
- Your details (name, contact details, availability and role)
- girl's name, DoB and address; and
- contact details of your safeguarding lead.
- Contact the girl and/or her parents or guardians as appropriate to explain the report, why it is being made, and what it means (unless you believe that telling the child/parents about the report may result in a risk of serious harm to the child or anyone else, or of the family fleeing the country, in which case you should not discuss it).

IMPORTANT - If a girl is in need of urgent medical assistance or you believe she is at imminent risk, act immediately – this may include phoning 999.

THE HOME OFFICE'S FGM UNIT

- Provides outreach support to local areas to support them in developing their local response to tackling FGM and to raise awareness of the unit.

- Identifies and highlights examples of effective practice across local areas and professional groups both through the delivery of our outreach programme and an FGM resource pack.

- Promotes available FGM resources including the multi-agency guidelines, e-learning, communications products (e.g. leaflets and statement) and resource pack which are all available to download from GOV.UK.

- Works with the police, Border Force, the Crown Prosecution Service and the College of Policing to improve the identification and prosecution of offenders.

- Has an overview of all government work to tackle FGM and works closely with the voluntary and community sector, survivors and professionals to develop cross-cutting policies and processes.

- If you are interested in receiving any outreach support or have any other queries, please email the FGM unit at **fgmenquiries@homeoffice.gsi.gov.uk.**

FGM PROTECTION ORDERS

An FGM protection order is a civil law measure which may be made for the purposes of protecting a girl[1] against the commission of an FGM offence. In deciding whether to make an order, the court must have regard to all the circumstances of a case including the need to secure the health, safety and well-being of the potential or actual victim. The court can make an order which prohibits, requires, restricts or includes any such other terms as it considers appropriate to stop or change the behavior or conduct of those who would seek to subject a girl to FGM or have already arranged for, or committed, FGM.

For example, the court may make an order:

- To protect a victim or potential victim at risk of FGM from being taken abroad;
- to order the surrender of passports or any other travel documents, including the passport/travel documents of the girl to be protected;
- to prohibit specified persons from entering into any arrangements in the UK or overseas for FGM to be performed on the person to be protected;
- to include terms which relate to the conduct of the individuals names in the court order both inside and outside of England and Wales'; and
- to include terms which cover individuals who are, or may become involved in other respects (or instead of those originally named in the order) who may commit or attempt to commit FGM against a girl.

Orders may also be made against people who are not named in the application. This is in recognition of the complexity of the issues and the numbers of people who might be involved in the wider community.

Breach of an FGM Protection Order is a criminal offence with a maximum penalty of up to 5 years' imprisonment. As an alternative to prosecution, a breach of an FGM Protection Order may be dealt with by the civil law route as a contempt of court punishable by up to 2 years imprisonment, a fine or both.

HOW TO GET PROTECTED

1) Where to apply for an FGM Protection Order?

An application for a FGM Protection order can be made at a Family Court in England and Wales. A list of court centres can be found in the court leaflet (FGM700) available at: **www.hmctsformfinder.justice.gov.uk/HMCTS/GetLeaflet. do?court_leaflets_id=12060**

There is no court fee for making an application for a FGM Protection Order for yourself or on behalf of someone else.

2) Who can apply?
   • the person to be protected by the order;
   • a local authority; or
   • any other person with the permission of the court.

3) Can I get legal aid?

Yes. Legal aid is available when you are represented in an FGM Protection Order matter including committals for breaching an order. A solicitor, or a member of a Law Centre or Citizens Advice Bureau will be able to advise on whether you have a reasonable case. Further information about legal aid and how to find a legal advisor is available either online at www.gov.uk/legal-aid or by calling **0845 345 4 345** (Monday to Friday 0900-1830 hours)

4) Can I apply for a FGM Protection Order myself?

Yes, or you can get a solicitor to do this for you. If you apply yourself you must complete the relevant forms and statements and explain your case to the court. If you need help to complete the forms, but do not know a friend or relative who can help, you should go to see a solicitor or the Citizens Advice Bureau. Court staff can help by explaining court procedures, but they cannot provide legal advice on the merits of individual cases or give advice about the probable outcome.

5) What forms will I need?

If you are the person to be protected or a local authority, you will need an Application for a Female Genital Mutilation (FGM) Protection Order (Form FGM001). This can be found at: **www.hmctsformfinder.justice.gov.uk/HMCTS/GetForm. do?court_forms_id=12000.**

If you need the court's permission to apply on behalf of someone else, you will need to complete an Application for leave to apply for a Female Genital Mutilation (FGM) Protection Order (Form FGM 006). This can be found at:

www.hmctsformfinder.justice.gov.uk/HMCTS/GetForm. do?court_forms_id=12050

All of these forms are free. You can obtain them from the weblinks provided above or from any of the court centres that deal with applications for FGM Protection Orders (a list of which can be found in the court leaflet FGM700).

To make the application, you will need to complete the relevant form and submit it to the court by post or in person. You can also send your application by email.

Further information on how FGM Protection Orders can protect you and the court process more generally can be found in the court leaflet (FGM 700). For more information on organisations and local services that can give you advice, please visit: **www.gov.uk/female-genital-mutilation**

6) What will happen when I provide the completed forms to the court?

The court will check the forms and give you a Notice of Proceedings for a FGM Protection Order (FGM002). This will tell you the date of your appointment before the judge. It is in your own interest to attend the court on the date shown on the form and you should be ready to give any evidence which you think will help you to put your side of the case. If you are worried about giving evidence in the courtroom, you should advise the court of your concerns in the application form. The court will decide what is appropriate, if anything, (for example screens to ensure witnesses cannot see respondents, video recorded evidence etc.,) in each case.

CLAIMING ASYLUM FOR FEAR OF FGM

Persons from abroad are permitted to stay in the UK ('granted asylum'), if they are at risk of persecution or serious harm in their home country. Not every danger a person might face back home enables them to get asylum. Instead, the UK government has set out a specific list, and only those can get asylum who face one or more of the listed dangers. Applying for asylum is complicated, and many people need help from a professional to do it.

Important things to know if you want to apply:

- You can only apply if you are in the UK.
- If you are a mother, you can if you apply fear for the safety of your child.
- There is no time limit to applying, but the longer you wait after your arrival in the UK, the harder it will be to succeed.

You will have to show the following:
- that you would be in danger if you were to return to your home country;
- that your home government cannot or will not protect you, for example because the police refuses to do anything to catch those who perform FGM;
- As part of your application, you will be interviewed. At the interview you will have to answer questions about you and your situation in your home country and in the UK. It is your chance to explain in detail the points you have to show, as mentioned above in the previous bullet point.
- While your application is considered by the government, you have exactly the same rights to healthcare from the National Health Service (NHS) as a UK citizen.
- As an applicant, you can request an interpreter and case workers of the same gender. The Home Office will tell you about all the services which you can use and what you are expected to do whilst your claim is being considered.
- Financial support is available. The Home Office will explain how you can apply for this.

HOW TO APPLY

- If you arrive at a Port (airport, by train or boat): speak to the immigration officer as soon as you arrive.
- Already in the UK: You must make an appointment with the asylum screening unit by calling the appointments line. Details are on the Home Office website at **www.gov.uk/claim-asylum/screening.**

More information can be found at:

- **www.gov.uk/claim-asylum/overview**
- **www.refugeecouncil.org.uk/languages** - This website provides guidance on asylum claims in 12 different languages.

USEFUL LINKS

- Multi-agency guidelines on FGM: **www.gov.uk/government/publications/female-genital-mutilation-guidelines**

- FGM: the facts (information leaflet) **www.gov.uk/government/uploads/system/uploads/attachment_data/file/482799/6_1587_HO_MT_Updates_to_the_FGM_The_Facts_WEB.pdf**

- E-learning course - Recognising and preventing FGM: **www.fgmelearning.co.uk**

- Procedural Guidance on mandatory reporting of FGM: **www.gov.uk/government/publications/mandatory-reporting-of-female-genital-mutilation-procedural-information**

- Fact sheet on mandatory reporting of FGM – what it means for communities **www.gov.uk/government/publications/fact-sheet-on-mandatory-reporting-of-female-genital-mutilation**

- Guidance and information on FGM including FGM resource pack for local areas and materials for raising awareness of FGM **www.gov.uk/government/collections/female-genital-mutilation**

- Guidance and information for healthcare professionals: **www.gov.uk/government/collections/female-genital-mutilation-fgm-guidance-for-healthcare-staff**

- eLearning for healthcare website: **www.e-lfh.org.uk**

FREEDOM CHARITY

Helpline

If you are affected by any of the issues raised in the book and you need to talk to someone, please call Freedom's Helpline on **0845 6070133.**

Freedom Charity App

Freedom's app can be downloaded for free and is available on all platforms. The app can quickly put potential victims, or those who fear for their safety, in touch with help and support.

The app also contains information for professionals.

Freedom Charity's homepage

www.freedomcharity.org.uk

Lesson Plans

Cut Flowers comes with PSHE Association accredited lesson plans on FGM.

Donate

Your support in raising awareness is crucial to help save lives of young people through education.

Just text the words **FREE02** followed by the amount you can give (£2/ £5 /£10 etc.) to **70070**. Or donate by BT MY Donate 'Freedom Charity 1139657'

Charity Registration Number 1139657

ABOUT THE AUTHOR

Aneeta Prem was born and raised within the sound of the London's Bow Bells and is a real life Cockney.

Aneeta's family originates from Himachal Pradesh, 'The Land of the Gods.'

She is the Founder of Freedom Charity.

Her debut novel, 'But it's Not Fair', has been donated to tens of thousands of children and has saved lives!

She was the youngest qualified female Black Belt karate instructor in the UK.

Aneeta is a Magistrate, chairing adult, family and youth courts.

Although based in London, Aneeta escapes to the country with her darling dog , Deeva!

You can follow Aneeta on Instagram, Facebook and Twitter @AneetaPrem and visit her on www.aneeta.com